Wednesday, The 12th
Late Morning

THE HEADSTONES WERE SPARSE. TO THE UNDISCERNING EYE, THEY were no more than a collection of small, flat-lying rectangles that seemed to be placed in no uniform manner. The names upon them were almost unreadable because of the brightness of the stone and the complementary shining of the sun. The months varied from stone to stone, but the years on the stones often repeated and remained unchanged within each small monument. Each one was a surprise to their living company who traversed them on this day that seemed to exist without time.

His ears were berated with the roaring sound of wind like driving down the interstate with the windows rolled down while he himself was still and outside of any automobile. If not for the migration of air, he would be utterly motionless as he stopped and listened to the howl of the ghosts of the past or present or future. The ghosts of what he did not know. The ghosts of what he pretended to not know.

He looked at the sky. It was a blue that made a person uneasy. So much sky and so much blue without a single cloud to break it up. All-encompassing blue, save for a single bird stuck in place

1

with wings stretched wide and body bobbing up and down. No progress granted. The lone man stared at the feathered beast through squinted eyes and wondered why. Why does it continue even when there will not be any ground covered? He thought that surely if the bird landed according to his passing whim, it would be blown away. As futile as fighting the wind may be, it kept one from being dragged away or covered by time. Better to be eroded than to remain intact and without will.

He often found himself philosophizing. There was a time when someone had been prompted by her observations to question why he thought and answered and spoke the way he did. The answer was not like his other answers, and it seemed to him that there was no other way to act. Why don't more people contemplate? Lofty thinking often, ironically, resulted in driving himself into the earth. Currently, however, the soil was much too hard for him to sink, despite the many little sinkholes south of a desperate amount of the ground-bound plaques. He was an unassuming soul among the ruins of life.

Being on the run was a curious thing. There is a constant, earned paranoia that persists in every single action one takes. In fact, this is also true for most situations that lead to these circumstances. However, in this moment, there was serenity as his mind cleared and thought of its current location. Finally, a man sought after; in a word: wanted. Here in this place, unmoving in vulnerability, he was safer than the wealthiest, most connected rat in the puppet world. There would only be one person in the whole of the world that would connect him with this place, and she was a woman more beautiful than she knew, who was far away from his life at this stage. Had it been months? Or years?

She had told him on a drive through this wide country about a grisly, unsolved crime that had occurred long ago. He thought he remembered her saying the '50s. A man had walked in off the

Worlds Separated

WORLDS

SEPARATED

A NOVEL BY

TYLER WILSON

JACKALOPE HILL

Cover art by Swifty.
Edited by Bill Stuart and Margaret Bauer.
Layout by Margaret Bauer.

The author can be contacted at therealtwilson@gmail.com

Published by Jackalope Hill,
The fiction imprint of Antelope Hill Publishing
Antelope Hill Publishing | www.antelopehillpublishing.com

Paperback ISBN-13: 978-1-956887-64-8
EPUB ISBN-13: 978-1-956887-65-5

You are closer to it than me.
I cut away parts of myself and put them into these pages.
Now, they are separate from me.
Now, they're yours.

highway into a family farm home and killed the entire family except one. The surviving teenage daughter ran miles and miles to the safety of the nearest neighbor. No reason was known, and the man was a stranger, at least as far as this highway-traveling stranger knew. The story had made him depressed. He had never gotten over it.

The furiosity of the Texas Panhandle sun was not to be ignored. His skin was beginning to burn and ache for the respite of shade. The air was drying him out and leaving a thin layer of dust over his body and clothes. He couldn't get over it. He smiled a little as he turned to walk out of the sacred grounds onto a ground that he considered just as sacred. Maybe he still felt freedom. He did not think he ever really knew the feeling, but maybe this was close to it.

Approaching the neglected vehicle that carried him loyally to this lonesome cemetery, Scott Austin took the keys from his jacket pocket and felt like an album cover to a heartfelt, heartland rock record. Typically American, or was it typically young? He had not had the opportunity to speak to a young person from a foreign land who truly embodied their respective national values. Accuse of him chauvinism, but he settled on American. Not all music was consumerist, he decided. Much of it was very much so and reveled in lowness, but some of it had genuine thought and ideals put into it. Less grand than the majesty of chapels and statues, but a shining example of human spirit breaking through what was merely economic to what was good.

As his thoughts on this matter completed, he turned the key in the ignition and cranked it against the firm resistance. The engine roared to life. When the shifter dropped into reverse, the radio finally tuned and began to play. A story of carelessness and remorse told by the well-worn voice of a widely-loved musician filled the cab of the plastic shell of the late model coupe, accompanied by the perfect amount of static to remind the listener that radio exists for the especially lonely.

While a voice filled with exhaustion serenaded the lone man, his eyes watched the horizon and the dirt path as it disappeared beneath his tires, cruising toward the highway. Speeding away from the summit between his mind, his soul, and the always speaking and rarely heard (and rarely heeded) voice of God, he entered the world again as he turned back onto the highway after a car moved past him at a speed unheard of only a century ago. The flash of the automobile paid him no mind, but he would need to be mindful of people once again. He had never overestimated his role in the world before this; now it was conducive to his survival to overestimate it in the extreme.

Behind enemy lines in his birthland, it was a time of heavy surveillance and pervasive misinformation, but the powers that be would certainly use their abilities to stack the odds against him in a way that would make the average, spoon-fed citizen kick his own dog out of contempt if it were known to associate with one Scott Austin. He felt badly for all the boys who had been given the name they now shared with him; children were cruel and there would now be a generation of Scotties and assorted middle names because of him. Of course, there was a possibility that he was only placing greater importance on himself than there really was. There wasn't any way to tell if they knew his name or what information they really had at all. Still, he worried about all these things as the tachometer climbed and dropped with his steady acceleration, trying to control his breaths and heartbeat with the consistency of the engine. Genuine humility was a death sentence for a man on the run. It translated to ignorance and obliviousness.

The wind shear rattled the vehicle and its occupant. Cruising two miles per hour below the legal limit, Scott tried to remember what the next town would be. His calf flexed with the precise movements of his foot, keeping his speed hovering between the two speeds he had selected. After the incessant advertisements of salesmen big and small, another song began to play. A drumroll leading into a swaying, lyrical experience for a name that reveled in its simplistic beauty. A song that he had not listened to at this stage in his life. A song that, when it spoke of loneliness, made his throat close; when it uttered the word "free," his jaw tingled at the hinge. Then the rural voice told him that he had been learning how to let go of a thing he had never held. With one hand on the wheel and one on his thigh, his knuckles whitened. He figured it must be the town of Turkey coming up and he could grab a bite there.

There was nothing more to do except go ahead and keep on going.

Tuesday, The 11th
Evening

THE RESTAURANT WAS PROBABLY FILLED WITH EVERY MOBILE member of the community, having quiet family meals. He did not stare or noticeably twist himself to gawk at all the decent folk around. Instead, he sat just quietly and tried to fit in as best he could as a single diner. He turned another page in the book he had picked up from a thrift store the preceding Sunday. The paper was yellow and rough like you find in all old paperbacks. The smell that lifted from each new page was that musty yet fresh smell that bookstores have. These young, unfettered words were seeing light for the first time in a generation comforted him.

He had grabbed this book among others to pass the time and sat down at the table with it to hide his face and make him seem easily passed-by. The prose had captured him. The story of the young, Welsh man enraptured him. The beauty of the land and language and people resonated with his own persuasions. His emotions raged inside of him like a storm he had learned about but never seen. His eyes would have given glimpses of the passion and his breathing would have become heavy, but he replaced his bookmark and laid it gently on the table to gather himself to order.

A chubby waitress slightly younger than Scott approached his table with a large smile and a wide-eyed, exaggerated look that let him know that she was trying to catch up with the world just like he was, or used to be. Her brown hair fell in wavy curls over her shoulder and enshrined the large smile that pushed up her heavily freckled cheeks.

"Saw-ree! I'm just about frazzled this evenin' tryin' tuh keep up with all these big orders!"

Scott looked around the tame establishment once again, smiling because of her stress that she created for herself.

"No troubles. . . . I waited . . . and you came just like you said you would. . . . I needed a little practice in patience." He always spoke with a subdued smirk and pauses long enough to make a person notice them but short enough that he could keep a train of words still connected, a side effect of his planning before action, thought before word.

"I hope I didn' wear on it too much! Whatcha thinkin' is ya fancy?" She had either perfected the speech forced upon people to pry money away from customers, or she was genuinely a bright person. Scott's cynicism said the former, but the small-town location and atmosphere pointed to the latter, and for that he was jealous.

"I'll just make it easy for you. . . . I'll have a water and . . . just a cheeseburger."

"Plain an' simple, I can manage that! Fries good with that burger?"

"Fries are perfect."

She spun and headed off toward the kitchen, checking on other tables as she went. He looked after her as she moved so spryly and swaying her hips. More than likely, she dearly loved the knee-length skirt she wore and saved it for busy worknights such as this. Waiting tables made her the focus of the spotlight, and she felt pretty and elegant swishing through the tables. Maybe it was vain, but that feminine spirit was honorable in a respective, equitable sense to the chivalry that men strive for. He replaced the book in front of himself so that it could comfort his nose with its scent of a feeble old librarian as frail as a page standing at the gates of Alexandria in defiance. Had the burning of libraries and their denizens set the world back by ages? Or had they stayed the flood of fire? If they had been filled with stories such as this one, which was injected with life and made his own feelings validated, certainly the former. If they contained other words of malice and unnaturalness, then the latter.

Lifting his eyes from the page that had commanded his attention, he considered the nature of things. How could everything be thought of so thoroughly and without misunderstanding? He swore that things were one thing or another, but they could also be so many things in-between. Could he be simplified to nothing more than an overthinker who became lost and confused in his self-constructed complications? Is consideration supposed to curse its adherents? Was his nonsense that of the onset of insanity? The pinnacle of it? Not thinking the way he did seemed madness to him. He started his reading again. At a new chapter, the bookmark was replaced and the book laid on a remote part of the table that was most likely to be free from any residue. Not long after, the careless, stressed-out waitress came flitting back and laid the basket in front of an unmoving—save for his eyes—Scott with a grandiose effort that was more than simple placement but less than a low bow.

"Hope ya enjoy, made 'specially for ya! If ya need anythin' else, just call for Jordyn!" The sparkle in her words let Scott know that was her name.

"Like the river?"

"No, more like the burger joint waitress," she spoke with a

giggle and the most expert wink he had ever seen.

"How embarrassing for me, I'll leave you to your duties, River," he flashed back after he had recovered from her wink, unable to return the gesture because his eyelids never seemed to want to cooperate.

"Now that's a pretty name," she smiled sweetly, an inward smile that forms when one feels desired, and turned away to continue her work, mouthing the word to herself and letting the sounds trickle through her mind.

"It suits you, then," Scott said low under his breath to lie with all the dead, kind words he had ever thought but had withheld. He whispered it as he watched her move away almost like she was skipping through a field in a fantasy, and he damned any person who would take that gleam away from her. There was only hatred harbored in his heart for whoever would be so careless as to suppress a love for the world and life so childlike and innocent that one cannot even feel contempt for the ignorance of evil. He held a drive to secure its existence because he himself had reveled too deeply in cynicism for too long to ever attain that purity.

The meal was unsurprisingly delicious and made Scott realize that *this* was true American cuisine, not the encroaching chains that tried to replicate it and spread like disease as much as they made people sick with their poison. This place was about food and feeding; the now-satiated young man could look around and see that. Even if he had not yet found the ability to point out specifics in his theory, he could grasp the feeling. The feeling was rich and welcoming, not sterile and financial.

"Save any room for somethin' sw*eet*?" She had returned and put forth a question that he had often heard, but this time it felt personalized for him as her tongue clicked resolutely for the high-note end.

Are you getting off now? Scott thought to himself, but instead

10

said, "I might . . . be able to manage a few more bites, depending on what my choices are."

"Welllll, we've got piiies and cobb-lers. . . ."

"I am *definitely* interested in the pies." He stared intently at her as she searched the ceiling for the available menu and droned her words instead of her usual pep in a way that a woman does to feign distraction to conceal her giddiness in regard to the conversation.

"Let's see," she said slowly as she tapped her chin and struck a pose, continuing to focus, "we've got apple . . . hmm . . . peach—"

"Peach?"

"Yeah, peach, aaaand chocolate," she finished reading the menu that existed only for her mind as her dreamy, ocean eyes settled back on him, a shipwrecked mariner.

"I've heard enough. It's been so long since I've had some chocolate pie. . . . Did the pie sweat?" he asked with raised eyebrows and a voice higher with excitement.

"Sweat? Whatcha mean?" she asked with the sudden appearance of a puzzled look on her face, while an uneasy smile appeared, ready to answer, but also weary of a stranger taking her for just some dumb girl.

"Like . . . the little golden drops of liquid . . . on the meringue. . . . I think it's sugar." Scott reeled in his enthusiasm so as to not frighten her and spoke quietly with a face relaxed back into tiredness.

"Ohhhhh," she perked back up, "our pie sweats profusely. Ya want the sweatiest piece we have?" She smiled knowingly and leaned back toward him from her place where she had drawn back in hesitation.

"That would be lovely, . . . please." His voice remained low, and his smile was less bright. Her reaction showed him that she had already been hurt. There was nothing undamaged in this world,

11

nothing left untouched by malice or self-focused people perpetuating the world's evils and shrugging them away when saying that it was "simply how things are now."

She brought the check and the pie at the same time with a bright smile. The slice was large and delicious, though not as special as one that would be made by a woman of his family. It had a different aura to it, a feeling that matched its home. The way she had said "enjoy" made him think that she liked speaking to him. Scott placed a five-dollar bill under the peppermill and took his check to the counter near the exit.

"How was it, sweetheart?" the elderly woman sitting next to the register asked as she gently took the check from him and brought it near her face to analyze it.

"It was very good." His arm felt heavy as it pulled itself up and lowered into the inside pocket of his jacket, removing his wallet.

"Well, we sure are glad to have ya. Whereabouts ya from?" Her hands looked fragile as they handled the cash that he handed her from the worn swath of leather.

"Ma'am, . . . I feel at home right here." Scott's eyes drifted to a small CD rack that had various country and folk musicians on display. He picked up one of a live performance that had been mentioned once on a lonesome radio station cutting in and out over the rolling hills.

"We'd sure be glad for you to stick around a spell then!" Her face brightened at his answer to her usual question.

"I would . . . if I could. . . . I think I'd like to take one of these too." He laid the jewel case on the counter and slid it an inch in her direction. She expertly punched some numbers in and his total rose.

"Shame, a new face would be mighty nice 'round here. But I s'pose we all gotta keep on movin' and ya cain't stop no matter how nice it seems any place. Not 'til you're sure it's home. That's how I ended up here," she spoke with a sweet epiphany, her head subtly shaking from old age. Scott was lost, and her eyes gleamed at him. He took a toothpick and set it between his teeth.

Several miles down the road southbound, the second track started on the speakers. Scott was headed out of Texas to a place he had never been before, with a feeling that would not let him alone.

Wednesday, The 12th

Dusk

A BASTION OF EXPERIMENTATION, THIS WEST TEXAS TOWN WAS. It really had not changed much from its foundation, despite the seeming evolution it touted as having undergone: the alleged evolution that was constantly undermined by people who felt rabid and snobbish pride at the sordid history, finding it a quaint little joke. After all, what was history but funny little stories? People did not really exist through the scum of it or drown in it; they were just forgotten, faceless characters.

The irony of his hatred of this place was not lost on him, but neither was it well-founded, as he did not necessarily hate the place so much as he hated what it stood for. A child born in Sodom or Gomorrah was not held to any standard of loyalty to his unchosen home. As far as Scott saw it, he could belong to the land and to God, but the only duty binding him to his home was the charge that he must not become part of it. He was born with the expectation that he had to change the place and make it a home for subsequent children to stand for.

Reds and oranges painted the buildings which were older than their owners, some of them holding nice local businesses, others derelict and beginning to crumble as a condemnation against those who feigned pride, and all the others filled with various flavors of drinking establishments for people to stumble out of and into the gutters. However, the street was quiet this evening, with business circulating through the restaurants and a nice ice cream shoppe. Families, friends, and young couples meandered around the well-lit streets window-shopping just for the experience and the company. Scott stood in front of a coffee shop which catered to and served as a major draw for the money of college-aged women who, like women of so many generations of that age group, were obsessed with, and threw themselves wholly into, the current trend. These times held aesthetics in general as the idol to be worshipped rather than appreciated like the creators of the art had intended. Individuals looked upon the area as something haunted and filthy, like its history, ignoring the craft and effort to elevate the lives the buildings served. They forsook the artistry of care for the glorification of immorality.

A pack of girls moved past the lone, ragged silhouette, giggling into the shop which smelled pleasant and looked clean, yet reeked of overpriced drinks that became status symbols in the eyes of young, spoiled women. Unfortunately, Jordyn would probably be taken in by the siren call of peer approval. As the sound of the girls disappeared and the door slowly fell shut, a bluegrass hit found its way to his ears: a folksy sound that made every person want to sing along because the words came so naturally. Scott leaned his upper body away from the metal column holding the balcony to the second floor of the shop. He straightened up and maneuvered the toothpick from one side of his mouth to the other and back with deft movements of his tongue. Maybe it was a nervous tick; maybe it was a conscious attempt at being cool. He felt both uneasy and cool.

Scott strolled down the sidewalk to his car and rummaged

inside. Reemerging with a small, thick device which held entire catalogs of various artists and many more partial discographies, he unwrapped a cord from around it and placed two loose ends into his ears. His ears felt empty with silence, a side-effect of a modern Pavlovian response. His thumb danced on the circular pad, clicking when he highlighted the proper title. With a final selection, he slipped the player into his jeans, the cord loosely curled in front of his plaid shirt. After a few seconds of silence, the strum of acoustic guitar began, followed shortly by the fiddle, and finally into those words which clung to the mythos of the wandering American. From Johnny Appleseed to the Western pioneers, to the romanticization of Bonnie and Clyde, was he now among those counted? He certainly wandered, perhaps in a general direction away from a certain point, rather than toward one, but that was the nature of wandering. To wander, one has to travel, and traveling is inherently between two points: the start, and the end.

While the assertions echoed in a large and lonely space, the body of Scott did its own wandering to the intersection and waited for the lights to glow white to cross, until he was on the opposite corner from the block which held his car and the giggling girls. Approaching the store, he gripped the handle and pulled, releasing a rush of chilled air, and stepped inside when the air had equalized and was no longer fighting his entrance. The haggard voice left his right ear as he approached the counter, removing the earpiece to hang down with the rest of the cord.

"Whenever you're ready," smiled the teenage girl between him and the dessert.

"That extra chocolate sounds nice . . . with . . . a scoop of the homemade coffee," the exhausted young man said with a bewildered half-smile.

"Cup or cone?" She had said these words in this exact order for as long as she was here, probably stumbling at the beginning, but gliding through the conversation at this late stage.

"Cup, definitely . . . please." Scott spoke with only glances at the customer service smile of the girl as he reached for his wallet and fished out the three dollars the menu said it would cost. She spun around and scooped the ice cream using the scoops sitting in the attached murky water. Why did they do that, and why did people ignore how unappetizing it was?

"That will be three dollars even!" She set the cup on the counter and smiled a smile that had been rehearsed a million times in a bathroom mirror, for people that she had convinced herself were not people she ever wanted to know.

"Thanks." Scott spoke quickly and handed the money to her, gripping the cup and turning decisively away and striding out of the shoppe. He had to get out of there and away from that smile which made him enraged and crippled with sadness at the utter severing of human connection. Just another woman peddling something, an occurrence not unfamiliar to these old buildings.

The ice cream remained untouched as he walked slowly down the block. He took a sharp right toward the river and the path which ran alongside it. Through a small parking lot, mostly deserted, shoes found gravel in a picnic area which he had never liked, where a bum slept on a nearby table. Scott cut immediately for the river and stepped onto a walkway of red, porous brick that conformed more to the Earth's natural disposition. He followed it down until it formed the bank of the river, beginning to spoon ice cream into his mouth, getting a portion in the concave area and slipping the utensil between his lips and pulling it out, repeating the process and getting layer and layer off of the slowly melting dessert, until, finishing that scoop, he went for another. It was a slow process, but it forced his body to take things slowly. Despite the tediousness of his chosen manner of consumption, mechanical movement took over and his mind returned to the feeling it had in the shoppe.

Like the giggling girls, the ice cream girl did not seem to exude anything but a form of the poisonous vanity pushed by society. Love yourself, except make sure to do it in such a way that would make Narcissus blush. Foregoing the debatable suicide, they instead live and snub others who would even dare to believe themselves worthy of such a presence. Ever since the world began there's been a thorn in the side of a man, but there's nothing so corruptible as the mind of a young woman; nothing so damaging and destructive as a young woman to a young man, too foolish to know that there be monsters, and those monsters are inconsolable differences between the two planes of life for man and woman.

With this admittedly misogynistic thought at the forefront of his mind, Scott broke away to avoid absolute misanthropy by stopping and setting his cup down and pulling out the box of sounds from his pocket. Touching the wheel, he searched for an album that brought feelings to him like he was sixteen again and he had just picked up a used CD: an original copy of one of the most iconic heartland rock albums, which had felt bulky in his hands at the time, case as well as disc, and had amazed him as every track played. But that was for another America: a naive one. This moment called for another album which had brought back those same exact feelings as when he first listened to the stadium-filling lyrics of that vintage masterwork. This contemporary album borne from divorce seemed a much more fitting comfort to a young man wanted and alone.

The silence filled him once more as the heavy little player slid back into his blue jeans and the cup returned to its place in his hand and the spoon replaced the sweet taste in his mouth. The sweeping music that broke the silence instantly brought about the feeling of hoarse pain that is innate in all people when they feel the distinct lack of affection in their life. Even the most outgoing, pretty woman can feel that lingering sting of being unloved when the broken voice of another relays their own story of being left or never having been found to begin with.

People seek out affective things, Scott decided. *Over time people just decided that the shallow feelings granted by instant gratification would suffice.*

An old memory rushed back to him of his time as Orsino. Surfeiting. Scott looked down at the sweating cup and recalled how he had understood that character. Understood him until the end, at least. Isn't it so easy to create such a simple mind so that there is a nice, clean ending? Or at least, happy in the mind of the onlookers. He had to stop placing people into categories. It was an easier thought that action, as he had never really been proven wholly wrong, except when he had tried to give one person the benefit of the doubt. Linear thought, as he had heard it put once. She neglected to realize how much the same she was, an exceptional mind falling right in line with what is accepted. The consensus. Democracy in America.

He thought too much. Scott stood still on the path, empty except for old men fishing, and tried to justify himself to himself. Or rather, to find ways he could be more defensible. Most of his life was spent in a sort of penance, trying to be good enough by his own appraisal. Harshest critic and worst enemy, and all the other clichés, which were becoming so watered-down that the original sayings had once again risen as beacons of lessons to learn.

Approaching a large, sinuous, water-level bridge, his eyes caught the gleam of something hanging in a tree, illuminated by the headlights of a passing car: wind chimes secured to one of the mighty branches. He made a mental note to hang a wind chime sometime in his life: another tick in a bucket list with few scratches, and many items rubbed away by time, forgetfulness, and a dwindling soul. Continuing to walk, Scott tossed his cup and spoon away into the first trash receptacle he came across, and busily licked at the annoying remnants of the ice cream which had evaded his mouth, eventually finding himself back among the dying remains of the aged town's once-bustling center. It was time to go as quickly as possible.

Turning his car around, Scott drove as slowly and as inconspicuously as he could. Coming to a stop at one of the veritable gauntlets of stoplights making up the grid of the downtown area, he spied a large pothole in the intersection. Under the ugly, grimy pavement was a red brick foundation. It was like replacing the ceiling of the Sistine Chapel with fiberglass tiles. His generational bias was cut deathly short and his heartrate escalated as his face flashed with blinding lights. Scott pulled through the now-green light, turning into a vacant lot, praying that it was only a bored, curious officer while popping his door from the latch that had held it tight for so many hundreds of miles so far.

The keyboard returned, the album looping in his ears. The car came to a stop and he carefully placed the shifter in park. The windows had already been rolled down to let in the night. The officer exited his car and began the short trek to the pivotal moment in his life. He was a very fat man and that would make Scott's work that much more difficult; hopefully he was tired or oblivious, anything that could be exploited. Loaded and ready to fulfill its use sat the snub-nose revolver in the caddy of the door.

"License and registration, please," said the officer laconically, his eyes looking over the car and at the weeds and shadows that populate an empty, urban lot.

"Right." Scott leaned toward the window as he reached his right arm in the direction of his back pocket. With a movement unhinged from hesitation, Scott unclipped his seatbelt with his right hand and threw the door open with his left leg and shoulder, into the officer's portly stomach, causing a deep grunt first with the hit from the door and a second one as he stumbled backward from the car, landing hard on his back in the gravel. Scott was out of the car in an instant, straddling the chest of the supine officer. Crossing his arm in a swift motion, Scott led his momentum by his fist, hard into the chubby cheek. Another punch came to the other cheek, driving the officer's head against the unflinching ground.

An unconscious uniform in the dark lay with blood trickling from the nose. Scott stood up straight and looked around, unsure of the shadows and weeds, just like the man before him. He ran to the cop car, tore open the door, and popped the hood. Scott held the hood open, knocked the connectors off of the battery, lifted it out of the Suburban, and let the hood fall closed again. The battery found itself a new home in the trunk of his own car. He still didn't feel confident, though, so he jumped back into the police vehicle and looked to the dashboard where a camera sat. He tore it off with all the force he could and tossed it in his trunk with the battery. Scott heaved the limp body of the officer toward the marked SUV and returned to his own. He sat in the driver's seat and buckled his seatbelt, sitting for a moment, acutely aware of how awful his hands felt. This was the first time he had ever punched any living thing. The tires crackled on top of the gravel and made his body jolt with the dip onto the beauty-suffocating pavement. Scott was so tired.

Does anyone still love me?

Saturday, The 15th
Morning

IT COULD ONLY BE DESCRIBED AS AN INTENSELY SURREAL experience, a different country, just a stone's throw from his home with a culture exceedingly its own. There were certainly aspects that leeched off or existed because of his own homeland, but what nation did not borrow and evolve? That was civilization, for better or worse. As things always are: better or worse. Scott let the toothpick droop from his mouth. If smoking hadn't always seemed so bad, there would be a cigarette in its position, but a thin piece of wood was a cleaner, cheaper, and just-as-cool alternative. His head no longer ached, but his right eye had a throbbing sensation. The pain couldn't compare to how tough he felt, though. He hoped that people were looking at him and thinking about him. That she was looking at it and knowing that it was for her.

Lilting, melodious sounds of the sweet song flowed into his right ear. Swarthy people generally lounged around the place. Sitting in the shade of a rustling tree, Scott considered the proper term for the location that had the noble purpose of beautification: park or square? Such a wonderful, social thing ruined by the reality of the world. For all of the peaceful, living frescoes of existence in this place, there was the staggering realization that people are paid to bring their bottles back to the store to combat littering, but that only means the streets, walks, and gutters are filled with bottlecaps. At least there wasn't shattered glass. What is life and the world when it becomes simply a list of "at leasts"? The dark eyes of the native peoples watched him with either contempt, curiosity, or courtesy. The ones of contempt from the modern people who wore their nationality on a jersey and did not look but shot daggers everywhere; the ones of curiosity from the eyes of children and young women who longed for his hair and complexion; the ones of courtesy from the old folks who hesitate before they say anything to the pale young man because of their habit of calling him and his kind *patrón*. He could appreciate all of the looks and their variety of reasons. Each in the proper amount makes for a strong person and a fruitful life. In a society killing itself, all of these were condemned as backward.

People in his homeland did not congregate as a community. There was no unorganized coalition of people sharing a place to live; a singular people with varying minds and hearts, but a cohesive experience. Parts of the culture Scott despised, but the fact that it was a genuine culture made Scott long for something similar. He swung his left arm at the elbow to bring his fingers in light contact with his toothpick, gently fiddling with it, reminding himself that he felt cool and trying to draw the conscious eyes of others. Especially the one who he was blind to at this moment with his eye swollen shut, blocking his side from view.

Finally, there was an agreement between the physical world and the way he felt: like a foreigner. It's so terrifyingly gradual how one can lose that feeling of home. There is no tragic ripping it from a person. There might not even be a slow death of what one knows. It is more of a realization that things are not as they seem. The nature of the thing is shallow, despite the metaphorical prophets pontificating that "all things are deep and rich, just don't analyze it," because doing so causes a person to determine the beautiful from the lacking. It stands as the elementary lesson in modern thought on art. A fallow field can harbor beauty in its sadness, but he and so many others had been trained to see only beauty. Then they had been trained not to see beauty but to merely feel good toward it. In feeling good toward all things, there is no need to scrutinize. Overthinking had replaced honest consideration.

The song began to slow and fade out and away when Scott felt a hurried jostle. The piano began again immediately, and the sad voice repeated the desperation of human thought entranced by the existence of another person. He felt the resettling of the petite physique out of his line of sight beside him as a voice small in force and statue was heard.

"I really like this song." Her timid voice barely swooped around to his unobstructed ear.

"The song . . . or the artwork?" Scott had a bad habit of smiling with questions that seemed pointed because he liked to drag the thought process of a person out so he could see it, and so the person being asked could, too.

"The artwork is pretty. . ." the confidence in her opinion wavered as she trailed off, "and I like it. . . ."

"Yes."

"But the song is very nice, too. I would like it even if I didn't see the artwork. I just saw the artwork first and I liked it. If I heard the song first, I would see the artwork when I went and looked for it to listen to it again." She spoke at length to all of his promptings now and Scott dearly appreciated it.

"So . . . the likes . . . don't influence each other?"

"No, they are nice all on their own. It's just nice that they are both really good."

25

She often used the word "nice," and the way she said it had a dreamy, trailing-off quality, which made a person think that she was absentminded, but she really used this decrescendo to hide her voice and make her statements ones that could be brushed off, betraying her own timidity and harsh self-critical nature that would scold her for thinking that everything she said was stupid, even to a man who had only taken every word as something golden. Scott had also learned about her and he knew that she fell so heavily back on this word because it was one of the few words she had been allowed in her past, a word that had not been followed by violence or screams, only smiles and nods. She had only been granted the ability to comment concisely and positively on things. Now that Scott had shown her an interest in her thoughts and ideas with which she was unfamiliar, her sentences relied heavily on the words that had been her friends for so long.

Her thin back and pronounced shoulder blades shifted against his bare arm. The cool fabric of the old button-up slid smoothly between the smooth skin of her back and the hairless underside of his forearm. Each time she made the slightest movement, her hair, which she had tossed back over the rear of the bench and Scott's arm, the strands of mid-length, golden hair tickled and pulled on the closely-related yet more auburn forest of hair on his arm. He felt so relaxed listening to her and the song, feeling the coolness of the morning and feeling her alive and not self-conscious beside him. He closed his uninjured eye and imagined her face and the infinite capabilities it held for expressing emotion and prompting it in himself.

The song started again. Scott whispered the opening lyrics with a bitter irony.

"I think," she began innocently before quieting her voice back to her whisper, "about you a lot." She spoke with absolute stillness, so that perhaps if these words were out of place, they would be attributed to another.

"When do you have time to think about me? We haven't been apart very much . . . for as long as we've known each other." Scott used a soft voice with a gentle smile to try and temper the harshness that his blunt words usually seemed to convey.

"I think about you when you don't talk and when I'm not talking. I guess my mind just sort of wanders that way." She was now speaking in the way that came naturally to her, swaying her head and shoulders to her sentences like they were sweet bars of music, and for the young man to whom she was speaking, they were.

"What do you think about?"

"You."

"What about me?" Scott smirked at her quick answer, which was only an answer and held no underlying sarcasm.

"Lots of things. . . . It's hard to say." She was still hesitant to say things out of place.

"Good things . . . I hope."

"Yeah, they *are* good."

"Any specific thoughts?"

"I think about how you are—" she stopped herself short, her inflection betraying that she had not finished her thought, before continuing, "so nice," she finally relented, almost whispering the word "nice."

"I didn't know I was nice," Scott lied. He did not lie in a malicious sense in that he truly did not believe himself to measure up to the definition of nice, but he knew that he was civil and had the habit of giving people the acknowledgement some people wanted, instead of the polite ignoring that many people practiced, because to them others had never attained an inherent value as beings in this shared plane of life and existence.

"You are the nicest person I've met in a long time."

"Who's the nicest person you've ever met?"

For a moment, there was thoughtful silence.

"My grandpa," she said with resolution dwindled by regret.

"Yes."

"I used to do ballet and sing when I was little, and he would take me to lessons and stay and watch me and tell me how proud he was. After, he would always take me for ice cream, and we would go to these little local stores that were filled with knickknacks that we would spend so long looking at." Scott felt the ache she did. The wavering of her voice was unmistakable. He sat still and dreaded that he might take it all in too deeply and begin to weep. "I would always wear bows in my hair because they are pretty and he would help me switch them whenever I wanted to change them out. There was one time that he found a tiny porcelain elephant that had a yellow bow right on the top of its head, and it had the biggest smile, so that its eyes were squished closed because of it. He picked it up and showed it to me and said it reminded him of me because it was so small but it was so happy, and I was so small and I made him smile like the elephant." Scott swallowed hard and turned his hand to hold her shoulder. The tears subsided. "He bought it, and when we got to the pickup he drove, he lifted me up, and when he got me buckled in, then he got in and buckled up, and he gave me the elephant. I pushed it back to him and told him that he had to keep it so he could be happy when I wasn't around." Scott felt the vigor drain from his muscles, stretched across the back of the bench. "He smiled so big at me and cried." Scott felt a few rogue tears dribble from his eyes.

"Yes," his word soft, and both of their bodies trembling.

"I—don't know—if he still—has it. He was so sad—when he—found out—what happened." Her tears were now impeding her speech as she would take desperate breaths after every few words, the memory wrecking her and the frustration making things worse as she could barely communicate.

"He does. . . . He still has it . . . and it means more to him than either of us could ever really understand. . . . You are loved still . . . even if you don't think you deserve it." Scott's voice was husky as he focused on his words and the drying lines on his face.

She turned into him, scrunching her arm with a bruised wrist in between their bodies and reaching her outside arm holding the media player across his midsection. She was tired, and he was sore, and they were both distressed. Yet, they were more at home than either had felt in a long time.

After several replays, she lifted herself from him and reached up to gently touch the edge of the discolored skin on his face. Scott flinched, and she withdrew her hand quickly. He turned to face her and picked her hand back up to touch the purpled skin and braced himself for the discomfort, watching her with an eye of understanding.

"I think about you a lot too." Her eyes shimmered as she held her hand very still, barely in contact with his cheek. "All wrapped up, up here." Scott touched his temple. "Are you hungry?" She nodded. "Let's go get some ice cream."

Thursday, The 13th
Noon

THE COUNTY ROAD WAS EMPTY AND BUMPY, AND THE FARTHER and farther Scott drove, the less sure he was that he was headed in the right direction. It wasn't until a mile later that he caught sight of the gray, metallic body of the single cab pickup. It was sitting proudly out by the road, slightly in the background of the neatly kept mailbox with a handmade wooden profile of a well-known cartoon dog dozing on top. The car stepped cautiously off of the raised road onto the slightly lower drive, the driver creeping up the path and feeling severely out of place driving an ugly, modern machine onto the property which had a pristine, taken-care-of look to it all. There was no overgrown lawn with abandoned farm equipment littering it and providing cover for all manners of critters.

Scott stopped his car in the place that seemed like the most appropriate patch of packed dirt of the drive to leave his hopefully soon-to-be-former transportation. The midday sun beat heavily down on the thoroughly exhausted young man and made climbing up from the low level of the driver's seat a particularly arduous task. He shut the door politely and walked across the dirt lot to the

31

sparse stones that made a path through the yard to the porch. The porch was one of the large ones with a swing and a place for a Southern belle to lean against the post and limply raise her hand to a departing lover. He pulled the screen door, which was little more than a formality, away from the house, exposing the entrance. Knocking on the carefully sanded and stained door seemed equivalent to sitting on a freshly painted bench or falling in freshly laid concrete, but it had to be done.

After his knuckles rapt for the first time on the heavy wood, the horrifying realization hit him that this was lunch time, and these poor people were probably just sitting down for their meal. His knock was too firm to hope that it had just been missed, so he brought his hand against the wood a second time, preparing his apology. There was a shuffling behind the door and the floor beneath him seemed to reveal extra weight which appeared through a feeling in Scott's legs. The door was masterfully maintained, and it opened smoothly and without any need for jerking motions to get it to come free.

Behind the mesh screen, an exceedingly thin body, which appeared frail came into view and looked at the young man with suspicion and hesitant curiosity, both being masked by a weather-worn face which had mastered the facade of grumpiness. Behind him came a small, mousy woman. She was much shorter than her husband and reminded Scott of something his mother used to tell him often when he was a boy: "You saw the world from behind my legs." The little, old woman had traded the legs of a parent or two for those of a husband.

"Sir, ma'am . . . I'm very sorry if I interrupted your meal. I didn't realize the time until I had already knocked. . . . I can come back a little later if that would be more convenient." Scott strained to see them through the mesh as the brightness of the land caused his eyes to be unsure of the proper pupil size.

"What do you need, youngin?" The old man's voice was scratchy and quivered like speaking was an exercise he struggled with.

"I'd like to buy the pickup you put in the paper." Coming right out with his goals seemed to be the right move with these folks. They both perked up.

"Well, come on in." The screen door was pushed open by a hand to a face which already showed more life. "Beedie always makes big meals that we can never finish on our own."

"I certainly don't want to intrude." Scott's mouth and stomach were suddenly empty.

"Nonsense; this little flower here gets tired of only having an old cowboy around to talk to." The aged man motioned him in, and Scott stepped into the dim, freezing home, his eyes adjusting quickly enough to see Beedie gleaming with love at the old cowboy who was using his bony fingers to walk the screen door back into place behind the youth.

The table was set with a meal fit for the prodigal son's return. It was a glaring mystery why this pair, who had eroded through the ages into one monument, were not at least sixty pounds heavier. The only connections he could make as he admired the scene was Thanksgivings from his childhood or a Norman Rockwell painting. In fact, the entire house, from what he could tell, was a capsule of what would have been vintage by the standards of the '60s. Everything seemed solid and natural. There was nothing cheap or soulless, despite every little thing that made up the home costing a fraction of what a lesser product today would cost. Scott felt himself pulled toward the chair that the smiling pair motioned toward, sliding into it and reaching for a roll. He instinctively withdrew his hand and looked down out of the trained shame when one forgoes his manners. Beedie squeaked and hurried over to him and reached across the table and placed a roll firmly on his plate.

"Go ahead and dig in, already blessed and all," she chirped happily, as she scurried to her chair that the old cowboy had pulled out from the table and pushed back in as she sat down.

The meal was conducted mostly in quiet, each person focusing on themselves and feeling the presence of the others. Scott tried to keep his eyes focused only on his plate, but he found his interest turning to the way his hosts were eating. Beedie ate like proper royalty, and her cowboy ate in a manner less dignified but still politely, yet they both ate very slowly. Scott thought himself to be a slow eater, but he had already finished half of his plate as the other two were finishing the first thing they had decided to eat. Almost three quarters full, Scott made sure his mouth was cleared of debris and glanced between the company, measuring their receptiveness to his prepared compliment.

"This is the most delicious meal I've had . . . in a long, long time. There is a great little burger joint up in the Panhandle . . . but nothing beats the time and care of a homecooked meal." Scott decided that he ought to speak his appreciation of the circumstances he found himself in.

"Thank you so much. Like Joseph said, we can never finish it all. Just a habit of making so much food when you're used to feeding a whole herd of hungry chitlins," she mused, her face shimmering with the opportunity to tell about her life and loved ones to a captive ear.

"How many?" Scott usually felt a certain twinge of stress when speaking to old folks because of their tendency to look at a person with hope: a hope that had died away from his own young eyes, which now only washed over his face with pleading for something better than what was to be found.

"Joseph and I have five of our own, and after that seven grandchildren and two great grandchildren." She beamed with pride, and the way that she said the old cowboy's name was with utter adoration.

"I dearly admire large families." Scott had civility in his voice, but he was hollowed out by the idea that these children were long gone from the arms that had rocked them, arms that now desperately grasped for something the world could not take away. In the darkness of the dusk of life, they must clutch each other and stumble together.

"So, you like the little pickup?" Joseph broke the smiling quiet of the pair.

"Oh Joseph, let the boy eat in peace without your money-talk," Beedie said, playfully expressing her exasperation.

"I'm sure he doesn't want to whittle away his day with a couple of folks time left behind; he's gotta get back out on the road," he said as his wife shook her head with a sigh, seemingly happy to have washed up with this man.

"Yes, I would like to buy it. The price you asked in the paper seems more than fair to me," Scott piped up to reinsert himself into the talk.

"Traditionally, a person tests and then haggles. . . ." Joseph seemed confused as he left the statement open for the guest to complete.

"Scott. I'm sorry I neglected to introduce myself. And I think of myself . . . to be from a different tradition than most people." He ran his hand through his hair and looked at the old cowboy whose face was not necessarily losing confusion but was certainly softening.

"We'll go for a drive after we clean up." He stood from his chair, followed by Beedie and began to gather plates, prompting Scott to follow the couple into the kitchen where they began the cleanup process. Scott made his way to the sink where he began the menial task of washing despite the protests from his hosts. Joseph scraped the food away into the slop bucket outside while Beedie stored away leftovers and then took up position beside Scott to dry the freshly clean dishes.

Joseph returned to the kitchen from the yard and reached between the two still working to wet his hands from his work. Soon after the old cowboy had disappeared behind them again, Scott felt the presence of a song. Some songs one can hear, but others a person can feel in the room. They exist like a phantom, passing through one while simultaneously lurking about, always eluding one's gaze. The voice was haunted and haunting, like a frightened dog, making its master afraid of the beast who would be his friend. His hands failed him as his washing ceased to be so deft. The homemaker beside him hummed lightly with a decibel reserved usually for use by a woman who would be drawing in ships to her sea-bound, jagged rocks. He felt the eerie lyrics slink across the floor and shackle his ankles, slowly vining their way up his legs and suffocating the natural breath of his body.

The dishes were completed. Scott dried his hands and followed Joseph out the back door and toward the road and the little pickup. The sun had not dialed down its attempts at arson against the Texan countryside. A speckled hand fished a mess of keys from the pocket of a pair of jeans that had seen a longer existence than the man not aged by years but by days.

"Here ya are, let's tool around." Joseph handed the amalgamation of keys to Scott with one held separately from the rest. Scott worked the key in the only way old keys and vintage locks seemed to function, pulling the key out and the door open. He hopped up into the cab and leaned across the bench seat, pulling the lock on the passenger door so Joseph could join him.

"It's all coming back to me," Scott said as he buckled his belt and fidgeted the key into the ignition.

"Familiar?"

"In a very comforting way. Just lower and a little heavier." Scott was being taken to a previous era of his life, which for some reason he was wont to do these days.

"How'd ya count that population?" Joseph had an elocution of the old cowboy persona that permeated him.

"My first car was an old pickup . . . bigger and older than this. I don't really know why, but the heavier and slower a vehicle is, the lighter I feel . . . so this makes me feel closer to that pickup than that little car over in your drive."

"Where is she now?" Scott was turning onto the country road, past the house in the direction Joseph pointed.

"Probably still sitting out in front of my parents' home . . . more than likely dragging property values down."

"Odd, that's what Beedie says every time I go sit out on the porch." Scott smiled a genuine smile. He didn't laugh, but he felt an overflowing emotion of appreciation at the old man's dry, self-deprecating wit.

"Would you look at that, maybe we are more alike than we thought," the young driver shot back, keeping his eyes on the ever-increasing horizon.

"*Gr-hmph gr-hmph.*" The old cowboy's laugh was gruff and hearty and real. "Careful we keep the windows down; we don't wanna microwave a couple o' cow patties like us. Sure can't smell too good, I'd imagine." The two men smiled at their own and each other's nonsense and cranked the windows low, letting in a cool rush of air. Both wondered to himself why they felt too self-conscious to do such a natural, freeing thing in the Texas weather earlier in the drive.

The drive conversation died down considerably with the battering of the wind against their eardrums, making their voices a tick in a pack of wolves. Joseph would occasionally point, and Scott would take the directions to heart. Winding dirt roads never seemed to end. The young man let his foot off the gas slowly, hovering the race of the engine until it came to an idle speed that crawled along the countryside. The cab became much quieter and was more akin to a turn of the century wagon than one with the power of hundreds of horses.

"Still familiar, Scott?" Joseph did not want the quiet to become uncomfortable for the young man, a man from a group of young people who always seemed to need to be talking or they would be overcome with nervousness.

"Takes me back to when I'd drive around with a golden retriever hanging out the other window." The thought was so vivid and close that he could almost grasp the feeling in the moment, but memory held it away and out of reach. The feeling could be remembered and viewed through the scope of the mind, but it was not the same. Feelings do not repeat, as far as Scott could tell. Trying to recapture a lost moment was futile and would only result in a manufactured, unsatisfying mimicry of what that piece of one's life really was. Every moment is different than the last and will never be repeated.

"Good breed, that one."

"She had the prettiest fur, all covered in cowlicks."

"Best breed, I'd assert." Both men were talking to the windshield.

"She saved my life once." Joseph perked up at this and turned to the young man, interested in the story.

"Let's hear this story. Go ahead and turn up here; it'll loop us back."

"It's not long. Pretty simple, really." Scott tried to quell any high expectations of his experience which he thought tame despite it being a possible end to his mortal life.

"Oughta be a refreshing change from the rest of the world then. Shoot." Joseph dangled his arm from the window and sunk low in the seat.

"There's a ratty old bench seat in my old pickup . . . and I had my wallet out of my pocket next to me because I had just gotten some feed. She was sticking her head out of the passenger window as far as she could. . . . We were sitting at a red light at a pretty heavy intersection when she decided to whip around and run over to me, knocking my wallet on the ground. . . . She went on back to her window and I decided to get my wallet off the dirty floorboards. . . . I bent down and grabbed it, and by the time I looked up, the light had been green for a second or two. I let off the brake and started to lurch forward. A dually truck that costs more than most people's houses barreled through the light at fifty miles an hour."

"Damn fool." The old man shook his head and his brain jumped across time and space to recall all of the times he had ever thought that, including reactions that preceded penance.

"The car next to me didn't go because they were turning left. The cars across the intersection hadn't crossed the midway point. The truck was in the lane closest to me and if I had been looking up when the light changed and went . . . I wouldn't be sitting here in this bench seat."

"Damn, damn fool." He shook his head more vigorously. "For better or worse, pard, you *are* here."

"Better or worse . . . never realized I was a married man," Scott joked, smirking at his stupid connection.

"The world is always there; marrying just means you're trading the world you know for another one." The old man was tired, but he was tired for the young man. Tired for all of those who did not know his happiness. "Not always, but we often tend to those the Lord knows we need—human or canine," Joseph grinned.

"She was the greatest dog in the world to me." Scott's face was grim as he thought back to a warm weekday home alone several years ago. Huddled away in his room, wasting his young moments until he had to leave for an hour. She had her bad days every now and again as she reached the upper echelons of the age of dogs, so finding her low in spirit on the kitchen linoleum, while heartbreaking, did not have a world-shaking effect on him. Scott had coaxed her into the living room to her bed so that she could have something soft to lay on. With her tucked on her large pillow, he had left. When he returned, with his father, she was lying in the threshold between two rooms, lower than before. The veterinarian was called. She was carried to the car and rushed there. A cyst had formed. All there was to be done was final. Scott held her. He did not cry. That night, he thought about it. The threshold in which she had been lying. She had been trying to find him in his room, but never made it. He had left her alone in her pain. Scott had cried profusely.

How could there be forgiveness for carelessness like that?

"How does it drive?" The old man posed as Scott pulled slowly back onto the drive with Beedie sitting on the porch: a sight the old cowboy caught before Scott answered and thought out loud, "look at the beauty in that scene."

"Looks like lyrics," dwelled Scott.

"My favorite song." The cowboy and his chauffeur climbed out of the cab and started slowly toward the porch together.

"It drives perfect as far as I can tell." The young man looked at his own boots beside the old cowboys as they stepped, disturbing the dust.

"Get ya where ya wanna go." Joseph waved to his wife as they crossed the halfway point of the lot.

"That's exactly what I need."

"You don't seem to need much convincin'." In fact, Scott was beginning to feel the paranoid pull of the hunted.

"I don't see much point in pretending I don't like it . . . or that the price isn't fair. I'd like to drive away with it today . . . and I'll even throw in the car I drove up in. There's nothing mechanically wrong with it; I just need . . . a change." The old couple scrutinized him with concern and Scott's heart leapt into his throat. He felt horrible dragging these people into his life. They had a peaceful little island away from everything, and here he was, building a bridge so that they could be plundered.

"I'm not really lookin' for a trade." Joseph rubbed the gray scruff of his jawline. "But I'll drop the price if you don't want the car anymore."

"No, no, I'd rather just pay you for the pickup; the car you can consider as good as abandoned. . . . I just need to get some of my stuff out of it."

"Well, in that case, give me a minute and I'll go and dig out the soft cap for the bed of the pickup. And I won't accept a dollar more than the asking price."

"You drive a hard bargain, cowpoke, but I'll fold for that." Scott's extended hand was gripped and shaken roughly with an ancient grin full of life.

"Go ahead and give Beedie the greenbacks, Scott; she is the financial wizard to the empire you see before you." Joseph stepped off the porch and began to shrink in the distance as he went to the barn.

"Let me go grab my bag with my wallet." Scott hopped down and strode to his car and then back to Beedie.

The money was counted out and handed to the old woman who set the stack underneath a glass of tea as soon as Scott finished handing it to her. Joseph returned with a rolled-up canvas with grommets and helped the young man to put it on the pickup, leaving a corner open for any of the traveler's things which he wanted to put there. Scott transferred all of his belongings to the pickup and sneakily slid the revolver into his waistband and stored

41

it back away into the pickup's driver's side door caddy. As Scott grabbed his sunglasses and the CD from the player, Joseph eyed the jewel case and trekked back to the house. When he reappeared, he presented the new owner of the old pickup with another jewel case. The old cowboy pointed toward the title track, and the young man climbed into the pickup. The old couple retreated from the heat to the shade of their porch.

Scott started the pickup and slid the CD into the player. As he looped in the lot and pulled past them, he waved to the bright, smiling people who waved back. The recently familiar voice poured out of the speakers, as haunting as ever.

In the rearview, there is a sight of an island. A kingdom of antiquity, untouched by the hands of greed and lesser life. Two individuals joined as one in manners that could not be fathomed by a foreigner's eyes. Living in a world separated from all that is left of the one decaying away. If Scott were to open up and tell his story, would they shut him away? Would they rejoin the world against him? Would they even be able to understand him? He had a world of his own, and there seems to be a lack of ability or right to comprehend worlds which are solely others'.

He stared back at them. The lyricist stared at a desired love. He wanted to reach out and hold that feeling that they held. The sad voice touched her. They faded into the back and disappeared behind the trees. The desired love disappeared into the trees. A man telling a story of worlds apart to a boy alone.

Friday, The 14th
Late Night

GETTING OVER THE BORDER WAS EASY. EASY, BUT TIME-consuming as it was probably the busiest weekly instance of exodus from his country into theirs. Nobody ever grew upset at a person bringing money into a country. Scott had probably gone overboard with his plan to make himself as barely-noticeable as he could, but it was not any concern now as the pair was shuffled through the checkpoint with the crowd of people who wanted to use this nation as a party destination that they could wash off after the weekend closed. She was a bit more relaxed than when he had first met her, but he could feel an underlying paranoia, like she was being chased. Is that the feeling he gave off to her? It was doubtful she could ignore her own pervasive feeling long enough to pick up on his, but then again, he had barely even learned her name. Bad situations aren't exclusive to the unintelligent.

"Do you speak any Spanish?" He asked her.

"Uh-uh. . . ." She shook her head in a subtle movement and spoke so softly that Scott wondered if her own answer frightened her.

"I hope I speak enough." At his cold words, which were not

43

meant to be, she shivered. While hardly perceptible, Scott noticed and cringed at his carelessness. There was a lesson learned: that an off comment like that can be construed as a snap at her own lack of ability. He would not be associated with the people whom she had known up until he had taken her away from them.

"Hey, Lily." He tried to force feeling into his blank voice.

"Yes . . . ?" The small voice barely survived the battering of the residual noise of the beginning of the weekend in a popular venue.

"What do you like?" Scott drove slowly through the streets just a few blocks from the checkpoint, the sidewalks and asphalt heavy with feet and a haze of a fast life.

"I don't know. . . ." She was struggling to open to him, or struggling to develop herself after having had her own self shut away.

"I like dogs and ice cream." Scott thought this sentence funny as he decided to say it with a wry smile, despite the joke being only funny to himself and not a single other person. With the right perception, an elementary pairing of words can have a sweet irony. And continue to only be humorous to Scott.

"I never had a dog, but they are nice. . . ." Her words, while still dwarfed by fear, seemed to come a little more naturally. "I like ice cream too. . . ." Lily would lower her head to speak to her feet and let her eyes return to the world around her while she was silent.

"I had this ice cream a couple days ago that was coffee-flavored . . . or some kind of coffee type of drink. . . . Anyway, it had shavings from coffee beans in it." The young man used esoteric hand motions to supplement his words for the quiet, motionless girl.

"Really?" she had perked up considerably.

"Oh, really, the unadulterated truth . . . and it was absolutely delicious." Scott took the opportunity to support her interest in it even though he could have done without the shavings himself.

"That sounds so good. I really like coffee-flavored things. They're nice." She actually smiled in a way that was close to her so that it would remain mostly hidden, but her body showed her smile.

"You are absolutely right . . . *nice,* simply delightful . . . *nice.*" Scott heavily accentuated his words so that they would feel sillier to her the way they felt sillier to him.

"What does that word mean?"

"*Nice?*" He swung his head toward her, raising one of his eyebrows as high as he could.

"Nooo. . . ." She followed her response with a girlish giggle, too new to his ears, prompting a smile from him before he continued.

"Unadulterated means that it's honest, genuine. It isn't sugarcoated or exaggerated or downplayed. It just is exactly what it is."

"I think I like all of those put together like that instead of that word by itself."

"But that would take a longer time to say. . . . I also don't think I'd be able to remember all those in that order."

"Me neither . . . but that other word is one I don't think I'd be able to say."

"Then just do it like this:" Scott brought his hand to his jaw and used it to control his mouth movements, enunciating through her laughter, "UN-UH-DULL-TCHER-A-TED." As her laughter subsided, Scott glanced back at her and coaxed her, "Well? Go on, your turn." She positioned her hand on her jaw like the young man across the vehicle had and stretched her mouth before taking a preparation breath.

"NNN-OOO."

She erupted in her giggling and Scott couldn't help but smile and shake his head. The wrinkles around the corners of his eyes did not dissipate as he basked in her gladness and tried to slow down every second of it for her. Eventually, it did begin to wane, so Scott tried to keep the banter going.

"You think you're real clever, don't you?" If winks were not such an arduous thing, he would have thrown one in.

"Heh . . . heh . . . ahhh . . . I don't know. I guess sometimes I am." Her animation was dying down in a natural way. Happiness and expression were not exercises that she was used to. It was obvious she needed to rest.

Scott found a street just off the main road that he could pull to the side of as he dug out his player from his bag. With the pickup placed in park, Scott found the little box and brought it out, the screen illuminating and straining his eyes in the dark. He handed the dangling headphones to her, her small hand cautiously reaching for them and placing them in her ears. He made sure the volume was an acceptable decibel before diving into the library to find the song he thought would be appreciated by her.

"This is good." Scott smiled at her as he selected the song.

The raucous start caused uncertainty to flash across her face, until she broke out in a grin when the instrumentals switched to an upbeat tempo that was akin to a soulful '60s song. Scott rolled his shoulders in a dance move as he smiled at her. Lily giggled and hid her face away from him in second-hand embarrassment. The driver's door flew open. A rough, large hand slammed him square in the chest before ripping him from the cab into the street. Scott forced his body to its feet outside of the pickup where he felt a fist like a train follow through against his right eye. He went hard against the metal frame of the pickup and crumpled to the ground, where he felt the moonlight hit him as the large figure took its shadow and disappeared. Lily screamed. Scott gripped the door and stuck his hand in the caddy, and pulled himself to his feet. She was screaming as the giant gripped her wrist and dragged her from the cab. Scott felt adrenaline course through him. He climbed into the bed of the pickup and leapt over the other edge with a small but deadly machine in his hand. The butt of the revolver cracked against the skull of the assailant. He yelped and went down, letting go of the girl who scrambled back into the seat of the pickup. The large dark shadow propped himself on his hands and knees. Scott fired the revolver resolutely, the bullet ripping through the dark hair and bursting the brains of the man onto the pavement.

The smoke slowly rose from the barrel as Scott viewed what he had done. What he had become. A murderer? Perhaps. But that would be decided in the eyes of those frightened. He looked to Lily. She was clutching the player to her chest, staring at the scene on the ground before her. Her fear was melting away as the look on her face showed only something that was more like curiosity. Scott would not attend to the condemnation of others. He was a man of action and they were not. Well, man of action, how will you react to the situation that you have taken and made your own? Scott lunged to Lily. Through the music.

"Are you okay? We have to go."

"Okay. Let's go."

Oh, a stray is not a stray to a man who takes in the lost soul, even though his own is sprinting blindly through a place where every turn is wrong and every end is dead.

Friday, The 14th
Late Evening

EVIDENTLY, THIS TRUCK STOP WAS NOT A HOPPING SPOT LIKE some places would be at this hour on this particular day. Besides Scott, there was a middle-aged truck driver who was angrily eating his meal, a cook who would disappear in and out of view of the window to the kitchen, and a waitress in a bright uniform carrying a notepad and a fly swatter. The large windows which looked out over a parking lot filled with sleeping trucks provided Scott with a decent view of things. In all honesty, he was quite inexperienced and naive when it came to this. If he was asked to tell about it, he could; if he was asked where to find them, he could tell that also; if he was asked to show where one was, he was at a loss. He assumed, with a fleeting hope, that he would prove to be lucky or impressive at reasoning, and most importantly, right.

"Whatcha want?" The waitress was blunt, but not necessarily rude, although her behavior would probably not instill very much confidence in her intentions.

"Just unsweet tea with lemon and chicken strips, please." Scott decided to play it safe as the waitress whapped the flimsy, plastic paddle against the table, ending the already short, disgusting life of a fly.

"You got it." She turned around and walked away, surprising Scott that she didn't try to ask if that was all.

The food came extremely quickly and was of appropriate quality. A safe meal is nothing to write home about, but it's certainly not a thing to undervalue. Almost finished, he caught sight of what he had hoped. At least he assumed he had. Through the streaked glass and bumping flies, he saw a young woman roughly shoved out of a car underneath one of the imposing light poles standing like a monolith with a forgotten purpose. She rubbed her arm and looked around; even at this distance, he could tell that she was nervous. Scott jumped up from his booth and shouted to the cook who seemed to be the only human being around at this point.

"I'll be right back!"

"Oh no, you leave some collateral, slick," the cook growled out the window. Scott, not seeking any more argument, grabbed his boot from his foot and tossed it onto the booth where he had been sitting.

Scott hurried across the lot, the pavement wearing away his sock and jabbing his foot. He hoped his irregular walk would make him look less intimidating and not more off-putting to the young woman as he approached. She saw him coming and instinctively took a step back from this zombie-walking insane person.

"Hey," was all Scott seemed to muster as he raised his hand slightly.

"Hi. . . ." she returned, shyly, apparently as unsure of how to continue as he was.

"Yeah . . . look . . . I don't really know how this works . . . or if I'm even right in what I thought . . . but I wanted to know if you could accompany me. . . ." Scott looked around quickly as he spoke, expelling each word as arduously as one could.

"I don't know. . . ." She was unsure of everything, from her words to her voice on the brink of disappearing.

"Oh, I'm sorry, I thought you were. . . ." Scott's face had flushed red and he began to back away.

"I. . . ." she stepped toward him with her head down, her shame in her own existence permeating every little sound and motion she made, "am."

"Well . . . would you mind waiting while I go pay for my meal . . . and get my shoe?"

"Sure. . . ." If not for the emptiness of the night, her words would have been crushed by the slightest, distant noise.

The young ideologue returned to the dining area, replaced his boot, and paid for his meal as the cook laughed heartily and the waitress glared at him. They had probably been audience to the awkward encounter in the parking lot. He returned to the young woman who had moved closer to the building and was glancing around at all the darkened eyes of the beasts of steel and rubber. She looked frightened. She looked like she was under the impression that the world hated her. She looked like she had been trained to think that the world was not hers for the taking. He felt guilty that she felt that way, despite his active working against the world that allowed young women like her to feel this way.

"This is mine." Scott motioned with restraint to the little pickup.

"Okay. . . ." She barely managed the two syllables.

"I don't really know how to do this, especially because I don't want something you're probably used to. . . ." Scott rubbed his neck. She shivered.

"I'm not used to any of this. . . ." Her shoulders drooped so low on her thin body that she could be another light pole in the lot.

"Is this your first time?" Scott didn't know why he was just letting his thoughts flow.

"Kind of. . . ." She made Scott feel large and unwieldy with her fragile speech.

"I just need someone to come to Mexico with me. . . . I can pay you and feed you . . . but I don't really have any way to get you back here. . . ." As he spoke, Scott gradually realized the reasonable and growing chance of denial.

"I've never been to Mexico. . . . Okay." She gently let the words fall to his feet.

"Okay? Really? That's great!" Scott's face lit up and he could almost swear that she cracked a minute smile at his enthusiasm. He ushered her into the pickup and tuned to a local station. With a smile still radiating from his face, he drove as the disc jockey's chosen track made him feel a certain nostalgia for a moment that in itself was memory of only fantasy. He had looked and he had found her. The crooning troubadour has lost her, and Scott had found *her*, as lost as she was. He was shocked at how informal she was, so undemanding. She sat quietly on the far end of the bench seat and hid a certain happy excitement as she was driven away from a fearful, lonely confusion into an unknown whose only promise was that it was not what she did know.

Over the waters of the Rio Grande, their souls danced to a song that would always feel forgotten.

Saturday, The 15th
Afternoon

ALTHOUGH MATERIALISM WAS ABHORRENT TO HIS DISPOSITION, he always held a guilty pleasure for second-hand items. Garage sales, consignment shops, or hand-me-downs: all sources were acceptable as long as the items came with a life all their own. The trip for the items was necessary, but his own bias drew him to a thrift shop as opposed to one of the many knock-off peddlers that dotted the storefronts, trying to attract gringo wallets. Admittedly, there were much less here than closer to the border, because fewer light faces were seen this far in.

Lily's small hand gripped his with their fingers intertwined. She used her shoulder to propel both of their hands in a swinging motion as they walked. The cord connecting the player to their ears extended between them as well, bouncing against Scott's forearm. It was something that would have annoyed him if he were alone, but he was quite happy with another reminder of living in this moment. Would it etch itself into his memory? Things he remembered never really seemed to make sense to him: walking on a sidewalk alone, not particularly observing the world around him in elementary school, a quiet card game with a family member he saw less times than the number of digits on his hand, a dead ladybug faded by the sun among some loose change, a living one holding desperately onto the fibers of his shirt.

He wanted to remember this moment. He tried to craft it meticulously in his mind so it would always be there to give him the feeling he wanted. It was a dangerous game, trying to create memories for oneself, expecting them to help in hard times, when they often exacerbate the pains of loss during the rough moments. Was he losing the moment as he tried to capture it and analyze it? Would being conscientious save or kill the moment? Did she enjoy the moment as much as he did?

The swaying cord carried the piano and American croon of a man making his soul shine through the earthly situations of mortals, assigning divine significance to every little occurrence that one happens upon. The familiar is so difficult to see as being heavenly, but perhaps that is why many claim to not know God. Scott's eyes had lost their focus and stared wide into the atmosphere looking for Him. Lily tapped on his arm, tearing him from the faraway clouds back to the moment. She pointed and Scott followed the path of her finger with his unobstructed eye to a store that had the look of a place they were searching for.

They walked through the open door, which made the store seem like a place that did not expect anything more than the nomadic type, the current pair fitting nicely into this generalization. The old woman sitting on a stool behind the counter looked at them with a smile, offsetting her droopy, brown face. She smiled at them like she appreciated their company toward each other for them. The two youths perused the store and found some ill-fitting clothes which would work for them in a practical capacity. With their arms filled with clothes, they approached the counter and Scott tried to communicate.

"¿Cuántos?" Scott said, forcing confidence in his single word, hoping that he was clear.

"¿Dolares o pesos?" She spoke back without hesitation, but with worry clear on her face as she gingerly touched her own eye. Scott could tell that she looked at the side of his face with an eye currently out-of-commission.

"Uhh . . . pesos." Scott shrugged as he made a general motion toward his eye followed by a dismissive wave to quell her worry and hoped he could figure out the amount that would be asked of him.

"Cien." She smiled and nodded with concern still washed over her wrinkled face, obviously as satisfied as a worried, but not pushy, friend.

"Okay." Scott clumsily tried to figure out how to give the money until the worn hand of the old woman reached out and began to count the money out for him. "*Gracias.*"

"De nada, mijo." She patted his hand with a smile.

"Necesitamos . . . to wear. . . ." Scott motioned to the clothes on the counter and to the clothes they were wearing.

"Sí, por aquí." She reached for Lily's hand and led her to the back with the clothes.

Scott shifted uncomfortably, not wanting her to be out of his sight in this unfriendly world. His heart was still at unease when the old woman waddled back out to the counter and smiled at him, handing him a cooled bottle of some fruity soda and holding it up to his eye.

"Thank you," he said without remembering to translate as he lifted the bottle gingerly against the inflamed flesh.

"De nada." She understood without issue.

There was no more reason to distrust a stranger than there was to trust. When Lily came hopping around the corner in an oversized tourist t-shirt and red jeans, which he could tell were cinched tight with one of the belts they had, he relaxed for a moment until he himself had to disappear from her sight again, holding onto the mischievous little grin she flashed when she saw the bottle on his face. Scott hurried into the best-fitting pair of jeans he found and used the belt to remedy the slightly larger waist. He slid into a decorative button-up shirt and rolled the sleeves, leaving the top couple buttons open so that he could feel the Mexican air on his chest.

As they left the store, the old Mexicana waved to them and said goodbye. The memory of two more nomads passing through her life would be hers now. Her world, visited by wanderers of the mind and soul, would continue until its natural end, surely. If she were to ever think of them after this lazy Saturday, it would be a fluke. Her world could not follow them and so she sat there, partaking in the worlds that came to her.

"I think I'll miss her," Lily said as their hands rejoined just outside of the shop.

"Do you know her name?"

"No, but she just seemed nice."

"You don't need to know a person's name to miss them?"

"I guess it makes it seem like you can't miss them if you don't know their name, but I think you can still miss them."

"How much do you need to know about a person to miss them?"

"I never thought about it."

"There's probably different types of 'missing' feelings, you know?"

"What do you mean?"

"Like there are people who are obsessed with celebrities and when they die people miss them. That's definitely not like missing a person you used to love and be loved by."

"That makes sense. I guess I don't miss her like I miss my parents."

"See, so how is it different to you?"

"I miss what I had and things I lost with my parents, and with her I just miss the feeling I had being around her."

"So, it's just a part of missing."

"Yeah, because that's all I had."

"The more you have the more you can miss. I miss things that I never had."

"I do too. What kind of missing is that?" She stopped and watched him as he stopped too, and the shuffled album looped.

"The worst kind."

He had missed her before he knew her. Who missed him? Loss was utterly wretched for making weary hearts beat with fondness for what no longer is or ever was.

OF ALL THE DAYS OF THE WEEK, NONE HAD SUCH A CRUSHING existential bent as Sunday had always had for Scott. He felt alone and wasting away each time he found himself on the Day of Rest at this hour. Maybe it was a cosmic punishment for his misdeeds and faltering in life, or maybe a weekly penance for only that week's sins. Just the way the bright sun shined, muffled through the curtains, made the room seem filthy despite it being no grimier than usual. The air tasted stale. The television played some *giallo* film from the '80s that seemed to sap Scott's strength each time he caught a glimpse of the hideous cinematography.

Scott had trouble seeing movies as anything besides movies. He saw the actors acting their parts in a scene; adults playing pretend. They were not in love, they were not superheroes, and they were not killers. Maybe some of them were the last thing. Probably the last thing. They were all liars, though. Professionally. Was it Aristotle who said something about that? Was it someone like Scott who would do something about it?

Fright was not a state of being in which Scott was well-versed, but at this moment, he was scared. He was scared of himself and of the future. He was scared of living. Troy was in the kitchen, probably doing another crossword in the big book they had found at the thrift store a couple of days ago. The previous owner had evidently given up on crosswords within the first two puzzles. It had pleased Scott that somebody had donated a used crossword puzzle book and it pleased him even more that Troy had bought it: a big joke to Troy and something poetic to Scott.

"What's a nine-letter word that ends in 'a' and means 'love of the past'?" Scott's assumption had been vindicated as truth.

"Nostalgia." Scott didn't hate the idea of the thing, but he hated the feeling. That pervasive notion of what is lost. That was nostalgia. Love was not the same as missing. They both could fill a person up, just in extremely juxtaposed ways. Love could be somber, and missing could be elevating, but when they were boiled down to their most basic elements, you found the same painting by different artists, using different canvases, different hair brushes, all different shades of paint, and with wildly conflicting strokes. Who was to say which was more preferable in the debate of highest art?

Sometimes, he would think about a word he knew, one of those foreign words that has no direct English translation, a word for a moment or feeling that would take an entire page of dense prose to explain, but once found would make the effort of description archaic, or merely an exercise in beauty. The word was similar to nostalgia in purpose, but it was specific to the feeling of loss that inherited the brief glimpses of happy memory; the things that were no more.

For some reason, his mind thought of Archduke Ferdinand. He could remember bits and pieces of the comedy of errors which led to the successful assassination of the leader, but for some reason, he began to think that he had never bothered to learn the name of the assassin who rocked the course of world events—at least enough to cause the actions and reactions of a countless number of others who contributed to the current state of things along their different developments.

The terrorizing face of the killer took up ninety percent of the screen as a woman screamed in the background. Scott leveraged himself off of the couch and stepped wearily to the bookshelf covered in dust and unread books.

"F . . . F . . . F . . ." Scott mumbled to himself as he found the red-bound books and began to search for the letter, as the collection was criminally out of order.

With the correct group coming into sight, Scott pulled it from its slumber and went and sat back down on the couch while the television played some of the gratuitous nudity which is such a staple in continental European cinema. He scanned the pages until he came upon the many Ferdinands. The Archduke among these had a biography much too short for even an encyclopedia, boiled down to the bare facts of one's existence; to be remembered for one's death. No sign of "see assassination of," and the assassin remaining unnamed solidified a dead end. Hopefully there was a history book on the mortally ignored shelves. The book was returned to its (incorrect) place and Scott scrutinized the other denizens of the wooden skyscraper until he found a book which hinted that it held the knowledge he sought.

In the beginning of the thorough account of the Great War, the name was given; a name he had never heard of. It was the name of a man whose existence was known by so many people; a man whose likeness and action were drawn in infamy in a sketch which littered books and historical circles. His name was unknown; an irrelevant detail to any surface-level discussion of the topic that is seen by many as a major shift in history. Being nameless was not something Scott wanted to be, but it was something he was nonetheless. Add it to the list, put an "X" where there should be something familiar, and submit it to those that count all that enters oblivion.

Maybe he was only fretting over nothing; maybe he was fretting over something that only mattered after the fact. Scott chuckled at the cliché of the thought which was annoyingly trying to insert its base-level self into his stream of ideas: the kind of idea that people who had never applied themselves to the act of thinking spouted and then moved on from. It is easy for them to forget so that they can have the empty epiphany in the future when God grants their mind the ability to wander beyond its realm without needing to have any of the concerns that come with adoption of new thought. Scott reasoned that if his thoughts were not like Samson gripping the pillars which held his world still and stout where he had always known it to be, he should not be satisfied with them. How foolish to leverage oneself into certain exhaustion and certainty in the ideas, truths, outlooks, values, or thoughts which was his near-hopeless goal in this commitment.

The exploitation film ceased to pollute the room as it came to its bloody, asinine end, leaving an absence in the stale, dusty air of the house. Scott turned off the television, entered the kitchen, and stood against the wall, watching Troy tap his chin with the eraser-end of his pencil to help him puzzle out the answer to the clue for whichever number he was working on now. He had not looked away from the book, but he had sensed the aura of Scott flowing into the room toward him.

"Good movie?" Troy still did not look up.

"It sucked. . . . I don't know what's wrong with the people who make those."

"Don't be so insensitive; it's called being Italian."

"That's no excuse. . . . Look at all the Spaghetti Westerns and how they're more hit than miss . . . shot for shot."

"Didn't you say that it was impossible to make a bad Western?"

"I didn't say impossible . . . but it is hard to mess up a Western."

"Right, right, and don't you also like slashers?"

"Yes . . . in a guilty way." Scott smirked as Troy pretended to still be thinking about the crossword, but he had not made another mark in the book since Scott had walked in.

"That was just an Italian slasher, a Jell-O or whatever you called it."

"*Giallo*, and that's exactly right. . . . It's an Italian slasher."

"So, the problem is that it's Italian."

"European is more apt, I think . . . but I don't know a lot of other European movies."

"American is better, evidently." Troy had almost have given up the ruse of continuing to think about the crossword answers to glance up to Scott, but he drew himself back into his mock focus.

"With slashers, yes."

"How?" Scott liked the way Troy asked questions. It gave him slight frustration when people asked something like "what's the difference" because it seemed a challenge of a person's knowledge in a way that did not leave the asker open to be enlightened to the speaker's way of thinking.

"American slashers are about purification, warnings against misbehavior like any boogeyman story. . . . European ones, or at least Italian ones, are just nihilistic. Degeneracy is the ruling force."

"Alright, alright, Leonard Ebert, maybe try somebody who cares." Troy liked to misname things for some reason. Probably the same reason the standing young man did it, just far more egregious. Scott had just gotten used to it and tried to ignore it, without correction more often than not. Otherwise he would be playing into his joke like so many others did.

"Going to actually write something down on the puzzle . . . or just wait for it to be ready to finish itself?"

"I was gonna wait until you came closer and I was gonna solve you, pal." Scott's face scrunched up in a silent laugh.

Scott sat across the small table from Troy, the wooden chair making a groaning screech as he dragged it out to sit. The two sat in general silence as the time ticked on and Troy filled in the squares and Scott read about the thing he longed for, and experienced: that foreign word. The language of the book's setting, even: the theme as a synchronicity.

After several pages and the completion of the puzzle, there was a clatter outside. The sun had lowered in the sky and was becoming hazy, but it had not yet touched the earth. An early, full sunset painted the dead grass of the yard as Troy had risen to go peer from the window. A sharply dressed young man exited a small, late-model vehicle and glanced around before he walked across the yard, staring at his feet. Roger halted and looked up when he stepped up to the front door and was greeted by the face of Troy as it swung open. The way that his face jerked into view, it was evident that he was nervous. Roger had always been nervous about everything. If one asked him if he thought the sun looked a little larger on a particular day, he would immediately become concerned that he had done something to mess up the size of the sun and he was being questioned about his involvement, and there were wrong answers that he could give with unknown and unpleasant consequences. What else was to be expected from a boy who had grown up under a father who was such by technicality alone?

"Welcome home, honey," joked Troy with the glee with which he always spoke to Roger.

"Yeah, Troy . . . right. . . ." Roger's normal laugh was tinged with stress.

Noting nervousness in a nervous voice belonging to a naturally nervous individual heightened the tenseness of the night. Scott was not nervous, but he had been afraid. Afraid and numb. Troy was the only one of the trio who had successfully hidden any underlying emotions for the night. Scott did not think that he was without any fear or doubt or nagging thoughts, but they were masterfully hidden beneath a bright personality.

"Do y'all want to tool around for a while until it's time? Or just hang out here?" Troy put the question to the room. Scott initially stayed silent because he did not want to influence his jumpy friend.

"We can go out," Roger sputtered.

"I'd really like to get out of this house. . . . I'm choking on the dust." Scott supported him.

"Rodge, you go ahead and get changed so you don't have to be uncomfortable." Troy stopped and tried to correct himself. "I don't mean comfortable, just dressed so that we don't—" he cut himself off again, feeling the futility of correcting himself to people who already understood him.

Troy grabbed some of the keys off of the hook by the door and went out to stand on the porch. Roger retreated into the bedroom to complete his task while Scott lingered behind, following him down the hall when the door to the room closed. Leaning his back on the wooden barrier to the bedroom, Scott looked at the ceiling with eyes like an innocent, curious child. He saw every imperfection that was visible from where he was. He took note of each one he saw for a reason he could not say. It seemed useless for him to do what he did.

"Is that you, Scott?" Roger's voice flowed through the door, the vibrations making it possible for it to be created being unfelt through the air. "Yeah, my wallet's in there . . . just waiting for you to be done."

"Oh, sorry. I'll hurry." Scott felt a cramp in his heart for making Roger apologize to him.

"No, don't worry, the slower we move the more relaxed I

feel . . . and I really need to just breathe." Scott rubbed his eyes.

"Are you alright, Scott?" Roger was nervous about anything he did, except for when it came to asking how someone was doing. Lots of people have one thing they really excel at, and Roger's was making other people feel like they were no longer shouting into the empty dark.

"Yeah. . . . I'm . . . okay." Scott pathetically gave a nonresponsive lie to a genuine inquiry of the state of his self.

"Alright, Scott." Roger knew it was a nonresponsive lie, but he could not reach out if he would be diverted. Instead, he just said his friend's name with his acceptance. Scott always wondered if he did it on purpose to endear himself to people, saying their names to them: the sweetest thing to a person's ears.

"How did today go? Anything interesting happen?" Scott hated how easy small-talk was, but with Roger, it always ended up as something intensely genuine.

"It was a regular day. I saw a cat on my way home."

"Is that why you're after your usual time?"

"He was sitting on a porch so superior that I had to stop. I walked right up to him and he only blinked at me and lifted his head a little bit, so I scratched under his chin."

"You walked right up to somebody's house?" The smile could be heard in all of Scott's words.

"I guess I did. . . . I hope I didn't frighten the people that lived there. . . ."

"I'm sure you didn't after they saw you were only paying your respects. Did *he* enjoy it?"

"He purred and grinned." And here Roger began his smile.

"Did you find out his name?" The door opened away from his back slowly, and Scott stood up and turned to see Roger in a t-shirt for a minor-league baseball team which was local to a small town in another state and an old pair of jeans spotted with orange paint.

"No, he didn't say, and I didn't think I needed to ask because I knew him anyway." All of Scott's questions were pleasant to Roger. His favorite thing about talking to Scott was answering all the questions he would ask. The wallet was passed from one hand to another.

Scott left Roger to put his shoes on and went out into the heat of the evening, where he found Troy now in the yard, climbing on the low tree which grew almost parallel to the ground. Watching his friend focus on the branch that held him, he pulled a toothpick from his pocket and placed it between his teeth. Roger came out and stood next to Scott, prompting Troy to hop down from his perch and start toward them as they stepped off of the porch.

"Who's driving?" Troy spoke first.

"If you're asking, and Roger just got back . . . I will." Scott held his hands out for the keys to be laid into his palm.

All three climbed into the car, Roger in the rear middle and the other two in the front. The ride was silent until a restaurant with a drive-thru came into view. Scott naturally gravitated toward it, and, with no voice objecting, gave an order when prompted. As Scott pulled around toward the window, Troy began his music, and leaned his seat as far back as he could until his face was next to Roger's right knee. The lyrics picked up immediately and closed off the ambient noises of the outside, unchanged world. They took stock of their food and counted their own shortcomings and limitations: the usual things that haunted modern man. Scott waved away the receipt and took the change. Howled phonetics begged them to wait for something that never seemed to come but never stopped looping in their heads. The boys took their food to a park, thoroughly abandoned by any functioning member of society at this hour of a Sunday. Conversation was a distraction from the thoughts of the night to come and guided them quickly to the end of their meal.

The group returned to the house after their meal, leaving the delinquent teenagers and their youthful loves to claim their park back from the invaders. Items were packed and transported and all the boxes for what needed to be done were checked. Troy pulled the RV out of the drive and Scott and Roger followed behind in the car. Scott asked Roger to play the song again. In his world, Roger reached out and turned on the song and heard it. Scott in his own watched him and heard something different. He had bided his time and it only ended a short while after it had begun: a love affair with a myth that he wanted to be a reality, but he had still begged for another dance so that he might serenade to life what had been embalmed well before he had met her.

Near to two similar men, yet inside he still felt alone.

Saturday, The 15th
Late Night

THE MOONLIGHT AGAINST HER SKIN MADE HER RADIATE AND illuminate the many-colored, pebble beach that warmed his bare back with the remnants of the hot day. Her arms burned against the stones and so she squirmed, not wanting to interrupt his serenity as he felt the same stones burn and leave their red marks all over his pale back. Such a welcomed low burn that penetrated through his torso and made it feel like the lake-air was forming beads of sweat on his cooking body. The moon was just a small, distant, perfect circle against the dark galaxy, but it created a spotlight on everything that the two young, hardly moving mortals could see. Shadows from the trees being thrown across their bodies made them look like a pair of exotic animals covered in a decorative coat of fur.

A sleek shine against the metal body of the clean pickup; sounds emanating from the cab. Words of remembrance and a synth to remember them with. Scott remembered what had been stolen from him. The silver spoon that had never touched his lips, but he knew that it ought to have been home in between his gums. Perhaps there was a less entitled way to communicate it, but he

69

did not care. The hatred against him had only ever fueled a hatred that, at its primal state, was that of a petulant child who had not gotten his way. They had taken the spoon, melted it, and formed it into some obscene sculpture. They had removed the practicality and injected it with scurrility that would medal it as the antithesis of what used to be good and right. Then it had been displayed as the only idol to admire and the only ideal for which to aspire. It had not worked on him.

And he remembered her, everything about her and how it was timeless. Faceless because it extended beyond the seams of his world and beautiful because of a perfect face. He could close his eyes and see her. He could write her name in flawless cursive in the etchings of his mind. When he opened his eyes, he could see her: in the moon and the trees, obscured by the shadows of the leaves, sprawled out on the side of the pickup where the metal was warped or dented. In the silence, she whispered to him. In the song, she harmonized. When he refused to listen, she echoed in his head. The world felt heavier than it did when he was without her. He could not float away like a lost balloon when she made his footsteps so weighted. When she made his movements so real, nothing could be light. Holding the air on his shoulders let him know that he did not exist in a vacuum. This was no black hole, but he would not escape her tragedy, their shared tragedy of existence.

The stones scraped against each other in that not unpleasant sound of crunches and shrieks as she lifted herself to a sitting position. Scott traced the stars with his sight until his view became filled with the light, her still slightly damp locks that hung over her oversized t-shirt with a dancing soda bottle on the front and some Spanish phrase in an inverted arch on the back. She tucked her legs up to her chest and set her chin in the notch formed by her knees. Scott closed his eyes and tried to imagine the view she had from over her thin legs. A still lake with a deep pearlescent

SATURDAY, THE 15TH, LATE NIGHT

color vying for attention when it was so often a person's habit to look upward for marvelous awe, instead of down, where they could see the distorted reflections of what they were used to. Was Narcissus so infatuated because of the distortions the water presented? A mythologist would probably vehemently correct and belittle Scott's curious considerations formed by his admittedly small knowledge on the subject, but his head was a haven from human criticism.

Scott lifted his arm from the stones and reached out to her back. He gently traced the foreign words which had been ironed onto the pale, mint green shirt. The upside-down exclamation point was something Scott enjoyed about the language. It allowed a reader to know before the end of the sentence how something was supposed to be read. Same with the question marks. In his mind he read the words: "¡Dale en el clavo!" His broken Spanish barely translated, and more than likely did so incorrectly. He thought "dale" came from "dar," and he was pretty sure that meant "to give," "en" and "el" were the simple "in" and "the," and "clavo" was something he had no idea about. It sounded like clavicle and Scott thought that was the collarbone, so he decided to say it meant heart even though he knew that was "corazón."

"Give in to the heart." Scott added a word to his own translation.

"I am."

"Are you happy?"

"I don't know. I'm scared."

"I'm sorry." Scott's heart dropped against his spine as his hand fell away from her back.

"Thank you for finding me and taking me with you."

"I thought you were scared . . . ?"

"I am, but I don't know of what. I used to be scared of things that I knew. Now I feel happy with things that I do know and scared of things that I don't know."

"Thank you for being here with me."

"There's something I don't like to think about."

"What's that?"

"What if you hadn't come to me? What if I had gotten dumped on some other corner?"

"I wouldn't have had the opportunity to be not angry, like I am with you."

"Are you happy?"

"I think . . . yes, I am." Scott looked at the mess of stars that made the sky less dark blue and more spattered, star-white.

"What're you thinking about?" Lily twisted her body to look at his serene face, unable to hide the thoughts of pain and anger that stormed behind it.

"I'm thinking about us sitting right here right now."

"What about it?"

"Nothing matters outside of this moment. We're here . . . and it doesn't matter how we got here or where we're going."

"I guess so. . . ." She hesitatingly expressed her non-disagreement.

Scott rose to his own feet beside her and walked to the water's edge, letting his feet slowly be overtaken by the pleasantly warm water. He slid his hands into the pockets of the ill-fitting jeans of which he had rolled the legs for this express purpose. They shared a space, but she was still a world separated. Maybe their worlds could be stitched together, but that takes cooperation, and sometimes that means mangling a part of one's own established world. It was probably impossible for two people to share a world. The closest one can get is living in someone's world at the sacrifice and abandonment of one's own, which, all things considered, was not as inherently self-betraying as it sounded. Some people needed to inhabit the masterful worlds of others, those of the highly intelligent and charismatic. That was getting into tenets that were far beyond what Scott had ever seen himself as. He didn't want to debate the merits of theories of existence and human relations because he could not comfortably take the stand which needed to be taken. He did not know where he belonged in that discussion. He only thought he knew what was wrong and what was right. He did not want to be the arbiter. He wanted to possess her, but he did not want to enslave her, to take her spirit as his own garden, not suffocate it on a leash.

"I just mean I would like to ... stay here with this feeling forever."

She stood up and came to stand beside him, locking her thin arms around his bent left arm.

"What's the feeling?"

"I feel okay ... a little hungry, and burned, but they aren't really bad feelings.... They feel good, with everything else. I think I'm actually, really okay right now."

"Is 'okay' a good thing?"

"Yes. It's not bad just because a lot of people use it when they are indifferent to things ... or want to hide things.... The real 'okay' is a very good thing and I can feel it right now."

"Have you not felt okay before?"

"Not for quite a while.... You make me forget the world and the past ... and myself." She nodded with understanding. "Do you think the things that came before and after matter right now?" She took a shallow, quiet breath for her confidence.

"Kind of. ..." she whispered.

"Why is that?" Scott laid his words with a tone of interest. She was like someone he used to know.

"I just think that things still matter no matter where you are; like it's all your life no matter what. I don't want to have only some things with me that will always be there, because it's *all* my life, you know?" She looked to Scott for a look or action of validation, probably assuming a level of intelligence in his thoughtful demeanor that conveyed the belief that he had already considered everything to its fullest extent. In reality, Scott had halted his thoughts to wallow in hers. The truth of the situation was that she was right. As much as he enjoyed not thinking about anything beyond this precise point in his existence, everything else continued with or without him. His soul was still stained, and others still touched by his past actions and even his current ones. Feeling okay in his temporary commitment to myopia was absolutely possible, as many people live their entire lives with the affliction, but he could not manipulate himself into thinking that it was disconnected. So much connection, but millions of different worlds. She could understand, but would she see a world that she had never known?

"I guess I just don't want any of that to ruin what I have now." He was somber and failing to conceal it. She put her head to his bicep as if to listen.

"But you still have what you do now," she pleaded.

"Now I don't feel like I have any right to have it . . . but I also don't want to lose it."

"But you do have it," she repeated, either to calm his thoughts, or because she could not fathom his guilt and fear in a way that she could condone or respond to besides well-meaning gaslighting. As foolish as Scott was, he did not think that he could not show her what he wanted to, so that she could understand him, but she may very well completely disregard the opportunity to be persuaded like many people are when confronted with a world they convince themselves is one not worth exploring.

"Right now I do . . . so I'll try to stop thinking about other things."

"Is that what you meant . . . ?"

"Yes . . . but don't worry about it. . . . I'm glad you understand now." Scott removed his feet from the water, ignorant of his dismissive tone when he spoke to a person who at this stage was the single most important person in his life. This callousness that is often too obvious after time has failed to close the bitter wounds it creates. He walked her back to the pickup which still emanated more of the same tortured voice over smooth synth.

Scott set Lily into the pickup and closed the door behind her gently, putting his body against it and pressing hard to force it to latch completely closed. He made his way around the front of the vehicle with his steps being akin to those of a wavering drunkard, his gaze cast downward. Inside the vehicle with the door open, he started the engine with slight difficulty that he had accepted and expected when he left the key in the on position for the music. Lily took the player in her lap and laid her hands, one atop the other, on it to keep it safe as it fed the music into the brand-new radio from the cheap, lengthy cord.

"You're not upset, are you . . . ?"

Scott blinked but did not see his eyelids. Through the windshield was the lake and night air that permeated the cab and intertwined with the music. On that pebble beach was the now memory of the time he felt really "okay," ignorant of the days that had plagued him, and the days that would seek to tear him down again. He knew that feeling couldn't last, but he didn't have that thought when he needed it so he could feel the "okay" even more thoroughly. Like an artifact in a museum, preserved behind glass, the empty beach was a painting. If he reached out to touch it, it would not be there. Was he upset? No. Was he okay? No. Why did he feel little things so intensely that they could ruin him, or make his body feel pins and needles of comfort all over? It didn't matter at this point. He wasn't a person that was willing to take pills for behavioral change.

"I'm not upset, Lily. . . . I'm glad that you're here . . . and that you speak to me. . . . I'm tired of so much silence that I'm so used to. . . . You're the noise I like. . . ."

She scooted next to him, her worries much more quelled.

"My grandpa would call me a broken record because I talked so much and I liked to do spins in my dancing." Her body made little hops like it always did when she got giddy talking about something.

"That's just because we can't stop putting you on that turntable . . . earning your grooves and scratches. . . ." She giggled and Scott put the pickup into reverse and focused his working eye.

How much of himself was he leaving on that smooth beach under a Mexican night sky? The tires lurched. Gaining a piece means a piece is lost. Synth accompaniment.

Wednesday, The 12th
Afternoon

SCOTT RECOGNIZED THE LOOK OF MUCH OF THE CHOCOLATE AND candy from vivid memories of his youth in now defunct convenience stores gazing at the selection. So much time spent perusing, but he would always leave with one of the same items as he always did. He had grown more adventurous as the years seemed to push by him, but he continued with things he knew he liked because it just didn't seem worth it anymore to go out on a limb—ironic thinking in the head of a young man evading capture, yet even his part and actions did not seem extremely far removed from who he was anymore. He had had his two friends to support him, and at the time he'd reasoned away the notion of the act being rash.

A small boy came traipsing into the aisle where he stood, simply staring at the selection and not really making any moves to choose. His appraising was entirely ignored by the little one who marched right up to the candy and scanned it animatedly, with his entire head moving along the shelves, his hands firmly akimbo and bowed outward like he was performing a children's dance. Without seeing the small, innocent face, Scott could hardly imagine the level of scrutiny being shed from his eyes. He had always considered the look of a child to be filled with awe and curiosity, but observing this action and then considering what he could remember of himself at that age, perhaps not all children are granted that outlook. Maybe scrutiny, caution, and distrust are the other side of things, or rather, just a recent development to defend against the evolution of the world and the society into which one is born, fighting to preserve one's own innocence since it hardly seems to be a consideration for the community at large.

"Hurry and pick something, Gregory." A low, female voice called both young males' attention to the end of the aisle. The boy nodded and turned back to the sweets while Scott lingered for a moment to take in all of the woman's appearance, having never seen her before. She was exceptionally tall, with the build of an Olympian or Amazon. Scott looked into her face which had harsh angles, but still seemed welcoming when she smiled at the stranger who saw her and returned the smile with one slowed and subdued by hesitancy, as always and for as long as she would live.

Gregory got down on his knees with two different items in his hands and looked at them, waiting for one of them to persuade him to choose either it or the other, depending on the motives of inanimate sweets which were a mystery to Scott. His small body showed the difficulty of the decision that was weighing on his mind. Scott almost let slip a suggestion, but he held it back. It was his decision to make and his alone. He would be responsible for his choice and the unrelated and sometimes unwanted things which attach themselves to it like a popular congressional act.

One of the items was thrust back onto the shelf as little hands shoved a body that was still learning its functions to its full height. Gregory began his movement with a skip that morphed immediately into a boyish run that represented a firefighter running through flames to a trapped family, a spaceman toward an invading Martian force, and anything else besides, through a slightly grimy convenience store to his awaiting mother to hand her a package of sweets, which she would then hand back after they were scanned. Little Gregory, like all young men, was running toward the danger that would make them feel like men.

Scott smirked, proud of the boy for making the steps he needed in the right direction. He only hoped that this microcosm of his life was not the outlier. One of his favorite treats was picked out of the box on the shelf and he made his way to the next aisle, displaying odds and ends for those on the move and in a pinch for simple, crucial things that would save time and decrease the chances of trouble. So much of it looked and screamed usefulness to Scott, but he could not bring himself to see any personal need for most of it. Perusing the various attention-grabbers, Scott felt his attention diverted to a television on the ceiling for any patrons that sat at the tables that were set along the wall of paned glass.

His eyes stared at a blank space of the metal dividing wall of the shelf, but his ears tuned themselves as his back tensed hard so that his muscles ached. He closed off his sight and breathed, relaxing his back and turned mock-interestedly toward the television screen. The news station was plastered by the heavily-painted face reading the prompts of an occurrence from earlier this week, identifying the bodies of two involved. Old pictures he had never seen before of familiar, smiling faces appeared beside the clown anchor. Still images would never capture who they really were. He could not look at the pictures and see anything other than his two friends, but he wanted to be able to know what other people felt when they saw them, when they heard about one action among trillions that make up just a singular day in the life of a person. Scott wanted to think otherwise, but it was probably hatred and condemnation of two people that he felt like had pieces of his world when they were told that they were monsters, flashing their pictures before them to show how malevolent they were. "Look at their smiles and know that they were going to come after you next." If a person had done a singular thing wrong in his life, he lost the ability to smile and be seen as a person experiencing joy. He missed them and he felt an anger build within himself at the mindless talking head dragging them through the streets to be gawked at, anger at himself for standing there and not being counted with his own smiling picture to make people who didn't know any better violently and erratically furious at the strange face smiling without grounds.

Their images disappeared. Scott swallowed hard and the color drained from his face. It had always been a possibility, but now it had become a reality. A sketch loosely resembling himself replaced his friends. The third man was being searched for. Any information on this individual was much appreciated. Scott laid the chocolate on one of the tables and turned to the cubby which held the restroom. He walked with purpose into the dim, dirty room, locking the door. His hands wrapped themselves around the edges of the sink in a death grip, his face contorted in pain and fear. Not pain and fear from a place of wanting no consequences of his actions, but a fear of the consequences he had fully accepted. He thought he had come to terms before, but now this hit him square between the eyes and forced his head toward the drain of the sink. Escape was doubtful. His future was gone, not that it was too terribly bright before he had gotten into this situation. He wanted to cry and vomit; neither came to grant him respite.

In the speckled mirror, a small, frightened boy watched him, a boy who had run into danger and found that deep masculinity that really made a man, and he had found the fear. Utterly terrified, he had run. The plan had always been to try and run to continue the fight for life as long as one lived, but he had run with his tail tucked between his legs. He had run away alone. There he stood in the

80

convenience store bathroom on the other side of the mountain that made men, and he felt afraid like a small boy. There were a million things he wanted to do, yet next to none that he could. The desire to scream and flail away from an invisible grasping hand came to him in a moment; he waved those thoughts away as he saw the fright in the boy's eyes reveal itself as expectancy. That boy would see joy again before the end of this, even though Scott knew that boy would probably not live to see the joy he sought for others. The decision was clear: abide.

Scott turned the cool water on low and ran his hands beneath it. As much as he wanted little to do with the water pouring from the faucet of this place, it would serve him. He ran wet hands through his hair and rubbed his eyes. There would be no concealing how ill he looked, but perhaps nonchalance would get him far. No matter what, he had to act as himself, he reasoned.

Exiting the restroom with and without care, he scooped the chocolate off of the table and approached the high school-aged young man with an unimpressed face behind the counter. There was not much to worry about from this individual, as Scott could tell that he only looked at the customer through the haze of whatever his preferred poison happened to be. Scott laid the chocolate on the counter and pulled out his wallet.

"And fifteen on the second pump." He delivered his rehearsed line with ease to the slow-moving worker who nodded and put the chocolate back in front of him.

"Yeah." The influenced young man looked at the bagged eyes and pale cheeks of the person he was serving. "You alright, man?"

"Long drive, and longer to go." Scott took the change from him and replaced his wallet, walking away and concluding, "no rest for the weary."

As the door dinged while he stepped back into the hot afternoon, Scott was noticeably self-conscious of the height indicators on either side of the exit and the cameras definitely watching him. Stilted to begin with, Scott gradually loosened himself and decided that there was no reason to change his plans at this point. He could have been more intelligent and stuck around to see what the media actually thought about his current moves, but ultimately, that chance had passed in his initial emotional reaction. He used the entirety of the money on the pump and washed off the windows, minding himself rather than deciding to look over every single person who pulled into the parking lot. It may have been ostrich logic, but if he did not care about who they were, why should they care about who he was?

Back in the car with the tank filled to the brim, Scott checked for the revolver just to make sure. A tingling fear felt its way up his arm as he felt the distinct shape. He pulled away from the awning that housed the fueling stations as he tuned the radio to something that would calm him and provide a re-centering of himself. Having no experience with yoga or zen or any real basic knowledge of Eastern philosophy, he made up his own calm center to find: a center which was inherently paranoid and suspicious, but at least it was himself.

A song from his sophomore year began after an old man finished saying something wise and worth listening to. Initial loves can be deadly to a young man who wants it to be his forever. Who knows if the man who penned the ballad to the acoustic guitar felt the same way, but a youthful Scott remembered his first true love. He thought he had her. She was already buried in a shallow, unmarked grave at the end of a twisted path that he tried to follow through the rain, waiting for a rainbow and not caring if there was any treasure besides her to take him in her arms.

He prayed for love and came out with an angry, pain-filled soul.

Sunday, The 16th

Afternoon

TOO MANY OF THE WORDS WERE COMPLETE MYSTERIES TO
either of their low-level Spanish skills, so whatever they ordered,
it would have a surprise for them. The best Scott could do was to
try and recognize the words that he could and maybe match up any
of the pictures that appeared on the menu with the items listed.
Eventually, the waitress returned to the young, pale couple with
their glasses of juice, neither having the stomach for coffee, and
Scott having warned Lily of drinking any water, just in case. Scott
looked at the name of what they had decided on and pointed to it,
looking to Lily for confirmation. Her big eyes did not break away
as she nodded her head like she was an enthusiastic student
imitating it from someone showing her how to do it. He relayed
the chosen dish to the waitress, indicating that the fate of the order
was to be shared between the two of them.

"I think the weather here is pretty." She spoke dreamily, using
her finger to sweep around some spilled sugar. Scott turned
around to look out the open French doors which led out onto a
generally empty and wonderfully ambient patio. The sky was a
gray that had deep impressions of black, separating each cloud

from one another, coaxing an expectation of thunder and lightning, or at the very least, a spattering of rain.

"This weather now or just the weather here . . . or this weather here and now in this place?" Scott dearly loved the subdued lighting that rainstorms brought, with the comforting rumble of something far off in the distance to let you know that the world was alive and beating its chest, and all one could do was to stand in wonder at the grandiosity of the things that have always been a certain way and would not change whether one were to run and hide, run into the open arms of it, or if one were to simply pass away while things went just as they always did.

"This weather and the weather here. All of it." She had become used to his oftentimes confusing interrogations into what she thought about things, because she had started to love them.

"What's different about the weather here than back in Texas? It's just a river between the two places."

"This feels different to me. It feels hotter and cooler and more everything. The nice weather feels nicer, and the bad weather just feels different."

"Not worse?"

"No. It just feels different. It's hard to explain."

"I think I understand anyway. . . . I think it feels different, too. The air is different here for some reason."

"See? I knew I wasn't crazy."

"You're definitely crazy." She swung her smile toward him. "But I get it."

"Then you explain it." She giggled at him, poking his forearm which lay relaxed on the table in front of him, tensing only as he maneuvered a toothpick through his fingers.

"Well, I suppose that it's not just a river separating the two places . . . that there's something in the ground or the air that makes a place feel like a place . . . in a specific, certain kind of way."

"I've always heard folk say that *people* make a place."

"People and places are different things." Scott shook his head and stretched his mouth out like he tended to do when he felt like something wrong was going on that he could not correct. "People can . . . make a place have personality, I guess, but . . . mostly they just make a place chaotic when they're there and peaceful when they aren't—"

"Or eerie," Lily pointed out, making Scott smile at her need to interject and to do it with a word he found weird.

"Sure, or eerie. The point is that people have some kind of effect that is only theirs and not a place's. . . . A place has its own feeling and . . . it's separate from people."

"Yeah, keep going." She leaned closer to him, intent on catching every word, smiling like she was truly interested as well as playing a joke on him.

"It's like when you're in a place that you are quite a lot. . . . Think of the normal people around it while you're there, and think about if you've ever been there alone. . . . They *are* different feelings, but the place is still that place. . . ." Scott's face lit up. "Like it's its own person that has its own feeling, but it isn't a person!"

"It isn't a person," she giggled again.

"It's a thing that's there and you can't talk to . . . but it feels like it talks to you."

"Now you sound crazy."

"I never once claimed to not be."

"That's great and all, but what does that have to do with why it feels different here?" She redirected his stream of consciousness back to the real topic like a sweetly condescending teacher.

"The point is that this is a place, no matter how big, and it feels different from the places we know." Scott released the tension in his body from his rambling.

"But we know different places, so how do you know?"

"I guess I don't know, I just think . . . we've got this place . . . even though we may never know what it's like without each other."

"I'm okay with that. I like knowing it this way." She grinned her school-picture grin, as big and wide as she could manage.

"Me too, Lily." Scott grinned his genuine, tormented grin.

The pair sat in silence, Scott with his eyes closed, trusting the world around him to the woman he was with, and Lily with hers taking in all that she could, hungry for the world that she could share with the man she was with. The waitress dropped off the food with a smile that most women make when seeing two young people, happy in each other's company: an envy which either manifests as or is suffocated by an empathetic response to emotional connection. The meal was not too surprising, though it was surprising enough for their foreign sensibilities, and they both would try small bits of unknown things before goading the other to join the adventurous one. As the meal came to a close, a simple flan found its way to their table; dessert apparently coming with their selected dish. While they lazily whittled away the sweet substance, there was a rumbling in the land beyond their sight.

"I *love* the rain. . . ." Lily whispered, almost hissing if her voice had a harsher feminine tone.

Scott set down his utensil and turned to look out across the patio once again. Small droplets began to darken the ground. Scott stood up. He could remember a time in his life when standing up at a dinner table or in a restaurant except to leave or go to the restroom was unthinkable. What was once taboo had no bearing on his desire to feel the different rain here, though. At the threshold onto the patio, he stopped and felt the change in the atmosphere that signified a storm's presence. Equilibrium was reached and he sauntered out from beneath the shallow awning, instantly feeling dainty, pattern-less drops wetting his shoulders and the top of his head, through his mess of light hair. Instinctively, he ran his hand through his hair once to fix it but withheld anymore attempts and looked straight into the sky. He had a goal of feeling the water on his face. Rain always felt different than ground water to him. It, with no lost irony, felt earthier.

"I love, too. . . ." Scott brought his head back to its default position and left his words hanging so that they could feel as loose and lacking in something as much as he meant them to. He felt a tug at his arm; he turned and locked gazes with Lily.

"They're closing the doors to keep the rain out." She did not look around when he broke his eyes away to see the waitresses and waiters closing the other French doors, and their own waitress standing at the ones they had come out of.

"Maybe they'll shut us out here with it." He took a final look at the clouds.

"I doubt it. She smiled too big when she looked at me and then over to you standing in the rain like some weirdo. Some weirdo American."

"I don't know how this place and people look at rain compared to how I look at it. . . . I'm not sure I want to know how they look at it. . . . I couldn't tell them about my point of view." He walked back inside with her, the door closing behind him by the hand of a waitress who could not help but to glance at his eye, and the dessert waiting to be finished on the table.

They finished the custard together. When the waitress returned with the check, they attempted to gain her help in paying for the meal, still mostly clueless with the monetary system of the country and how everything worked. Eventually they were successful in their transaction and rose from the table as the waitress strode away to relax, since they were the only patrons who seemed to be at any of her tables. The rain outside had picked up considerably, constantly distracting their attention to the French doors which were not well-enough protected by the awning to stay dry. It came down heavily in drops that you could hear beating the surfaces they landed on. The building felt much cozier with the harshness of inclement weather outside: the purest definition of shelter.

As the pair walked between the tables and brick pillars, Scott felt the rain transplant his body to a different place and time. Some familiar place during a familiar, comforting time, as he sat in his childhood home with parents who harbored an unconditional love for him. The windows were shut but the blinds open to a windy, rainy evening. He remembered that going to stand on the porch to smell the petrichor meant a commitment that would result in one's legs below the knee being spattered with water. It was one of those memories that means a lot to a person, even if it was probably lost to oblivion for everyone else involved. It exists as a thought that no other living person has because it holds only significance for him, and he does not know why. The front door was down a short staircase, beset on both sides with high walls that at the top were no taller than waist height, but it served as a suffocation point before the openness of the dining room floor or the crushing vastness of the outside world.

"It's coming down so hard—and so much." Lily peered out the window of the right door of the doubled entrance.

"I thought you liked the rain?"

"I do, but when I talk about rain, I mean rain; I don't mean swimming without the swimming part."

"The pickup is just over yonder, see?" Scott pointed to the vehicle through the bushes and wrought-iron fence.

"Yonder." Lily giggled at his down-home diction.

"Like the mountain folk say." Scott grinned, proud of the word.

"Like my grandpa would say." She leaned against him.

"Ready to run?"

"Not really." She blinked at the monstrous clouds.

"Do you want me to go get it and pull around so you can hop right in?"

"Definitely not." She wheeled around and faced him. "I want to stay with you."

"How long do you plan on doing that?" Scott looked intensely at her serious, unwavering face.

"I think you know." Her words shattered the noise and the silence to create its own. She swallowed hard as her face broke down slightly, frightened at her assertion that came from a place that recalled a guillotine, with Scott holding the lever. In his hands, a shared world on the precipice of birth and death, founded by a scared, lonely heart.

"You are my place." Scott gripped her arms as he squared their bodies to each other in that small entryway, providing his breath and soul to keep the newborn world glowing with the signs of their own Eden.

Lily began to weep.

"Oh, Scott—"

He embraced her, his lips meeting hers softly; her lips, having found his, pushing against him in desperation to be closer. He dropped her arms and threw his arms around her midsection, pulling her where she wanted to be, the place where she belonged. Her hands finding his face to caress. Tears streaming down her cheeks and wetting his rough face as they met in the throes of the passionate kiss. After an undetermined amount of time passed in the world outside of their own, they broke away from each other as gradually as one is wont to do when one does not wish for something to come to an end. Scott looked at the streaked face of Lily and spoke as gently as he ever had with her.

"Let's go."

"I'm with you." She looked toward the world.

He pushed the door open for Lily as she scampered out into the torrential rain, following her out, but making sure the door closed securely behind him. She did little hops in the rain as she waited for him to catch up to her, a mere few feet away. He got to her, and they started to briskly jog toward the pickup. Their joined hands swung as they moved until the slack in their arms started to disappear, with Lily pulling ahead and feeling a force holding her back. Confused, she turned to see Scott making a show of taking slow, exaggerated steps.

"What are you doing?!" She delightedly yelled, her hair a shade darker and twice the weight by now.

"Look, I'm not as good 'a swimmer' as you." He took another, large and heavy step into a growing puddle.

"You're crazy!" She began trying to drag him by taking hold of both his wrists and pulling, wearing a smile that did not fade while her eyes blinked and squinted to keep out the consistent rainwater that tried to invade them.

"I'm soaked, too, don't forget that part." Scott smirked at her as she made faces from her efforts in trying to move him.

"You are el lunatic-o." She dropped his wrists and stepped back, looking at him and waiting for him to say something.

"Hey, Lily." His voice was low and nervous.

"Yeah, Scott?" She met his tone with her own.

"I. . . ." He stopped and breathed deeply, either reconsidering what he was saying, or taking a moment to criticize himself for having so much trouble in saying it.

"What, Scott?" Her eyes pleaded with him, her chin quivering.

"I love you."

She was expecting it, but she wasn't prepared for it. She froze initially, in a standoff with the young man with the rising and falling shoulders. Her face looked almost hurt, and it killed him.

90

The world ignored them and continued to pour on. Their world posed, perched in expectation. He waited for anything. He had made his move, and now his was hers. He could not undo. He could not regroup to make another move. The progress of it lay with her. She was scared. She had no prior experience with this, an honest expression that lent her the power to hurt.

She broke into a run toward him. He reacted and planted himself firmly. She leapt into his arms that made her seem like a snowflake flittering without care for whatever direction may be down. He caught her in his arms, prepared to hold the weight of all their world, but felt like he would almost fly away as she presented no burden to him whatsoever, save for a slight tinge in his face to remind him that he had already proved to himself that he was willing to fight for her. He had used his words because they were precious to her. She responded with action because it was the only thing that meant something to him.

The water made them shiver and cling together as they buried each other's faces where shoulder met neck. So many meaningless words spoken by others melted away from him like dripping wax, running down to a new wick to begin a new life. The careless, self-serving actions of others fell away from her like the winter coat of a wild cat prepared for a new season of its life.

Scott lowered her to the pavement which had become one large puddle and walked her to the vehicle. He set her inside and entered the driver's side to find her already in the center, waiting to be near him. He pulled his wallet from his pocket and set it in the floorboard to dry. Leaning over her to fish the player out of the glove compartment, he felt her lay her hands and head onto his back, and he felt loved. He selected a song and turned the defroster on; both of them were soaked through to the bone, but close to each other's hearts.

The instrumental began slow and true and quiet. And then

there was a quiet, feminine voice not unlike Lily's. A song for you from me, whoever you are, and whoever I may be. A cover of the original to prove that point. A true serenade, walking the lovely and alone through every chord. She hit repeat when it began to fade.

Under the rain, we love.

Saturday, The 8th
Evening

"ARE WE SURE ABOUT THIS?"

Scott looked to Troy and Roger, waiting for a response, gauging their body language and the way the eyes could sometimes betray one's thoughts. Of course, he was having second thoughts, and certainly they were as well, but he wanted nothing to be left unsaid. They needed to consider every single thing before venturing into this. While he harbored doubts, he was also pretty confident in his whole commitment to things. He just liked for his friends to talk and thereby make the situation so much more real.

"Let's talk about that." Troy was usually the first to speak up or respond to anything, unless he felt like his stake in things was less significant than someone else's.

"That sounds good." Roger concurred with his friends.

"I suppose I can start, seeing as how I never really stop," Troy began, leaning back in his chair, his hands resting on the top of his head. "I'm ready to do what we need to do. And that's how I see this whole thing: an ugly need. I have wants that are different from this, and wants that are beyond this, but when I think this over, I can't see any of those wants coming true without this need."

"What if it doesn't work?" Scott posed the question to Troy. "What if it's futile and we do it for nothing, or worse, less than nothing? What if nothing changes?"

"That's not the point. It's a possibility that this is all for nothing, but it's not a guarantee." Troy shifted his weight onto the table, his elbows propping himself up. "My wants are strong enough to take that chance and to accept the consequences either way. At least I'm doing something. I don't want to sit around like a zombie while I can feel myself caged up, worried about what's next because it's out of my control. Look, I know that this is entirely a risk, but I'm okay with that. It's probably selfish, but I don't want to die for nothing, and even if nothing goes the way I want it to, I died for something. I died for myself and for something I wanted."

Scott set a cashew between his teeth and dragged it in with his tongue, watching the unmoving grain of the wood table at which they sat. He chewed in a way that allowed his ears to reverberate with the crunches, thinking about how the sounds were made and wondering if his friends could hear them too. He could sit here and repeat this action until the world decomposed around him, but that would keep him right where he was. Nothing would change. Troy was talking about change, about progress toward a goal for a better future that they all shared. After all, he thought, wasn't festering in a place unmoved one of the most painful, dishonorable things in which a man could find himself? Sisyphus may be the embodiment of the definition of insanity, but his active role surely made it more bearable than the alternative. Holding the boulder partway up the mountain meant that it would fall no farther, but it also meant that one could never know if the boulder would remain at the top this time.

"This will affect a lot of people." Scott retrieved a toothpick from a nearby box and placed it on his bottom lip.

"Anything worth doing is always that way. If you want to change your life, it's always going to make waves. For people that used to know you, people you do know, people you haven't met yet, and often people that will remain strangers, but they feel the ripples. Like that old movie you like." Troy pushed himself back again, raising a hand to Scott as he passed on the personal connection meant to communicate his point, something he only did when he was afraid of being misunderstood.

"I know. . . . I just can't help but think about all the doubts I have." Scott removed the pick to speak.

"Go on, say your doubts." Troy looked expectantly at him while Roger looked primarily down, glancing up every so often.

"Hear me out," Scott began. "Maybe 'doubts' isn't the right word, but it's just a thought. I'm committed to it at this point too, and not in an unwilling way, but I just keep thinking one thing. . . . Will people understand us? Will they just hate us because they think we're wrong? I can see where they find wrong with what we're going to do, and that makes me hesitate. On the other hand, I look at the way they live, and I *know* they are wrong, so I have to do this. I can't help but think that they'll never think about it like I have."

"They don't need to think. They have other people do it for them." Troy sounded genuinely distressed, or perhaps furious. The truth can cause more anger than anything else, it seems, because he was exactly right. No matter what happened, the majority of people would tune into whichever station or individual to which they had handed their moral authority to see how they should feel about a particular thing. Not even the act of thinking, just what guttural emotional response their brain ought to activate based on the tone of voice or the look on the person's face as they delivered this silver platter to their masses. Troy started again. "I'm not convinced that we'll have any effect on anyone."

"Like you said, we're doing it for ourselves, when we come right down to it." Scott tried to comfort his friend who was now visibly experiencing the thoughts that were plaguing him when he brought this conversation to them.

"Everyone can stay right in that handbasket like a bunch of happy idiots, but we're breaking out." Troy began to get worked up, waving his arms, increasing in volume, and leaving an empty quiet when he ceased.

"I shouldn't have—" Scott began to try to defuse the distress he had spread when Troy cut him off.

"I'm glad you did. I needed to do more thinking so I'm not like the rest. Now I'm more convinced than before."

"Is that all you are?" Scott did not intend to sound so harsh when he saw the betrayed look on his friend's face.

"No. I'm also unsure of why I have to be like this. I hate myself for needing to be like this." Troy hit the chord that Scott didn't know he was feeling and trying to communicate to them. To tell the world that he often wished that he wasn't like this, so that he could just share the simple, blissful, empty worlds that so many people look like they inhabit from the outside; a world where the grass is greener in that valley of monomania. Scott drew in a breath, searching for the confidence he did not need to talk to people who would die for him.

"Besides anyone that might already think the way we do, there's only one person who won't hate me after this," Scott finally mustered.

"Who?" Troy asked, but in a manner in which it was difficult to tell if he was lost in his own thoughts or just somber.

"My mother." When Scott talked about his parents to other people, he always said mother or father. Directly to them he would use mom and dad, but he couldn't bring himself to call them that to others. It felt childish, and the archaic forms seemed to place them in a much more respected position to the people with which he referred to them. And that was a position in which he was certain that they belonged. Why shouldn't good parents be hailed as champions in times of broken homes and immature adults? However, that is all he said. How can it be said in a way that isn't insufferable and embarrassing that one feels like a disappointment to one's parents? Putting the blame on oneself was never really easy when the moment came, and there was to be no blame assigned to the people you truly felt had done no wrong. It was a barbed knife that stuck in a person's stomach, and one did not want to call attention to it for fear of anyone that listened to attempt to pull it out.

"You shut up about that," Troy failed to stutter in his hiss. Scott stared in disbelief. Perhaps in all of his perceived shortcomings, he had come further than a peer he admired for being so put-together. Where Scott struggled emotionally was down a path his friend had not been able to trek through lack of capability or fear. Did confidence come from absolute personal-emotional knowledge? Or did it spring from the at-home feeling one can find in the emotions of others? In his friend, he began to see the latter.

"Are you alright?" Scott looked concerned at Troy, who had lowered his head significantly from its usually high position, and caught a glimpse of Roger's face in his peripherals, showing his full consciousness of his surroundings.

"Look, I'm fine. I—" Troy began harshly, but quickly softened, a realization of his embarrassments being met with understanding, "I'm sorry. Can we just forget that?"

"Right, no problem," Scott assured him, the killing of intimacy leaving the empty feeling of losing something that cannot be retrieved.

After a short, contemplative silence, Troy and Scott had both returned to their usual, respective states. Gathered, Troy looked to Roger who felt his gaze and met it. Troy's eyes narrowed on Roger and simultaneously brightened.

"Personally, I'd like to hear from the wide-of-vision, impressive-in-ability Rodge." Troy smiled encouragingly to his nervous friend.

"I'd say that there were two of us," Scott seconded the motion.

"I don't have much to say, guys." Roger shrugged off the attention.

"Oh no, you're not getting out of the question like that, not with us. We know you." Troy slapped the table and pointed at Roger with a smirk.

"Come on, Roger." Scott coaxed in his usual way, a way that he worked tirelessly in order to sound like a person who could hear what was said.

"I've thought about all the things you guys said and I thought myself." Roger always stopped himself before continuing his thoughts, always making sure they were wanted. He did not want to give where it would be an inconvenience to all involved.

"Yes?" Scott acknowledged for both he and Troy.

"I think we are all here because we don't belong." Roger's face was carved seriousness. "We don't belong to this place or this time. I don't know if we were never welcome, or if we got kicked out of it, or if we removed ourselves." He looked to both of them. If they really hadn't known him, they would be stunned; instead, they were thankful he was giving them his words. "All my life I've felt like a mistake. Not like some clumsy nobody, but like I was somebody, but that I was missing my time, that somehow in this cosmic mess God had misplaced me. Accidentally putting somebody important in a place or body where he could never be important." He checked the audience again. "But here I am. And I know that this is important, and it's because of three important people. I'm all in, and I don't have a single doubt in my mind that this is supposed to be any other way. This world wasn't meant for us."

Each young man looked at one another, their thoughts and judgments of the others pulsing in their eyes like wild animals ready to attack. If they had not been close friends in agreement, one would only assume the natural progression of events would lead to a bloody brawl. Scott knew that Roger had already had the concerns they expressed to each other a long time ago. It was foolish to think otherwise. Of the three, Scott may have spent the most time lost in a maze of thoughts, but Roger was a different thinker. He thought about things more critically than Scott did by leagues.

Scott remembered a conversation he had had with Roger several weeks prior. He had brought up to Roger the fact that psychologists would probably revel in diagnoses of the three of them latching to each other and planning something of this sort. He remembered specifically how Roger had become angry at the thought. Withholding his desire to rant on the topic, Roger had said that it didn't matter how they diagnosed them or even if they correctly guessed their motives; it did not make them any less legitimate. "That was the whole problem," he told Scott, "that people thought guessing reasons for doing something made them any less than they were." And Scott was glad he said that, because he had unconsciously thought that way too, until then. When a child wants to play with a toy to keep it from a peer, what difference does it make pointing it out? The child does not wish to share the toy with his or her peer; they are just expressing their desire through a more tactful action than outright saying that they do not want to share. It does not change the motive, nor does it inherently make his or her want wrong because his or her underhanded method was seen for what it was, meaning that they have learned the lesson to be even more tactful in the future so as not to be called out.

"And you were going to hold that in? Unbelievable." Troy jabbed at Roger who gave a slight smile.

"I forgot how to speak English, temporarily," Roger joked, looking down.

"But you remembered," Scott pointed out.

"Some days I could swear he was born dumb." Troy shook his head.

"Some days I wish he had been, when he decides to be smart like that." Scott continued the good-natured abuse with Troy as Roger grinned.

Conversation grew lighter as the time passed. Roger suggested a game of brainteasers that Troy wholeheartedly agreed to. Scott played two rounds before deciding on a walk. The greatest irony about him was that he hated the lonely feeling he had, but needed to be alone to organize himself and his thoughts. He picked an apple from the fridge while the harassments from his friends to remain quieted as he closed the door, setting the buds in his ear and waking up the device.

The pavement had met his shoes by the time he had located the song he wanted. It began as it always had, as many times as he listened to it after discovering it. "This world wasn't meant for us." Roger's words had strangled him and were showing no signs of letting up. No breath would pass freely as long as those words rang true. Homeless and world-less, dreaming of that ideal home that evaded their lives while they took shelter from the fire and rain in worlds their own. He wasn't sure what Roger had meant by that, but he was damned sure of what it meant to him. Scott had felt it every day of his short life without the words arranging themselves in that way to describe it. A ladybug, late in the season, landed on his shirt. Was he home for the little, curious creature? No, it didn't belong. Just like him, it was looking for something, but just holding on for dear life onto a massive body hurtling through things it didn't understand. Except that couldn't be; it fought for survival. It did not fight for a future.

The lyrical poetry settled on a familiar thought, repeating it with greater feeling and crescendo. Scott felt the words inside, and focused on an icy exterior. There was no use in self-pity, and there was a fine line between self-appraisal and self-pity: a careful balance for all things human; a balance that almost no man seemed to maintain, much less even reach. He could not hate right now. It would take too much out of him. His ladybug flew away.

He had found a couple of friends that were willing to burden themselves with him, and every creak of their backbones was a reason to continue.

Monday, The 17th
Morning

THE GATE WAS EXTREMELY BUSY, WITH THOSE LOOKING FOR work and going to work making their way, and Scott hoping that they could successfully blend into the rush and make it back over the river without consequence. Their youthful and haggard appearances would ideally create the facade of having slept off a crazy weekend and just returning home—which, for all intents and purposes, they honestly had. Lily lay on the seat beside him, snoring occasionally. Scott kept the windows up and the upbeat, still heartbroken music low, both to drown out the noise of the world. Not the world, but the society that made all the noise. Crowded and stressful, Scott inched closer and closer to the checkpoint. The singing poet assured his love that they shared each other's mistakes. Scott waved away a skinny Mexican that tried to start washing the windshield, only leaving after Scott held his finger to his mouth and pointed to Lily. Another few feet closer to the checkpoint and he began to really feel the weight of the stress.

"This was a mistake," he barely whispered, his words dissipating into the roar of the air and the sway of the melody.

He looked around nervously; there was no way out. Too many people driving too many cars were forcing him forward to his own defined doom. He tensed up so hard that his muscles shivered from their over-exertion. The line was moving quickly, and the uniforms moving around the vehicles toward the front set him on edge. There was nothing illegal in the vehicle except for himself. They had evidently crossed a threshold where dark-skinned vendors were no longer moving in-between the cars. The guard waved the line forward.

Begrudgingly, that was the way his foot came off the brake, allowing the wheels to carry them to the guard post. So much seemed to be going on around them. Scott slowly rolled the window down, not due to the feeling of being cornered, but so that the cab would not jostle and wake Lily. He looked up at the guard with the long face and buzzed haircut and gave a greeting smirk and reached for his wallet.

"Where you headed?" The agent leaned over and scanned the cab, stopping on the still ripened purple eye Scott wore.

"Home. It was a nice weekend, but it's time we got back where we belong." Scott had pulled out his driver's license, just then realizing that he had not been asked for it, nor was it a passport. He felt like he was going to be sick.

"Seems like a crazy weekend to me." He motioned to his own eye and did not let Scott respond. "Just the two of you?" The long-faced man seemed nice, holding out his hand for the driver's license which Scott relinquished.

"Just the two of us." The romantic pop tunes continued to hum in the background as Lily shifted, feeling the change in temperature and hearing the voices.

"Long drive ahead, I see." The guard handed the identification back. Pointing to the eye that could not see the finger, he asked, "Gonna be alright to drive with that?"

"Not really; that address is my family's permanent address. I'm staying here for now, and this shiner is on the way out." Scott saw no purpose in trying to shorten the interaction or lying. Both would be suspicious and that was not within his survival budget.

"Really need to get that changed, then." The lawman ran his eyes over the truck and Scott caught sight of his partner walking around the perimeter of it.

"I would if I was in a more permanent place than I am right now. Move around a lot." Scott tried to give as much information as he could without lying.

"Your friend?" There were beads of sweat dripping from under his hat as he motioned to the young woman sleeping on the other three-fourths of the seat.

"Oh, right." Scott gently touched her thigh and spoke softly. "Lily . . . hey, Lily. . . ." Suddenly he felt a touch on his shoulder, and he turned to see the guard waving away the need like a troublesome fly.

"Anything to declare? Plants? Animal products?"

"No, just some second-hand clothes." Scott looked intently as the guard looked toward Mexico.

"Alright, have a good one." He looked toward America and waved Scott on, who began gently rolling up his window.

He laid his hand on her calf. Scott did not know what was going to happen, or what he was going to do, but this felt like a final act: the last movement of a symphony; the final strokes of a brush against a canvas that renders a painting complete and the artist empty. His immediate mission to return to the soil from which he had sprung had been successful. There was something lacking without the steady march toward uncertainty. Had he become some sort of adrenaline junkie? His sickness had subsided, and he could breathe, but his lungs were not working correctly. The black hole in his soul phased into the world and took everything away from him, and he wished to cry out to be fixed.

Lily sat up and rubbed her eyes, yawning before looking around to see where they were and if it was familiar.

"Here . . . put your seatbelt on." Scott switched his eyes between the road ahead and the belt on the other side of her, grabbing it and pulling it across her before she took it from him and secured it.

"We're back." She was looking around like a curious little mammal, not in danger, but wanting to see.

"We couldn't stay there forever." Scott drove, weighing his options.

"Why not?" She ran her hands over her thin legs from her thighs to her ankles, making sure they had the blood they needed from being curled up on the seat.

"We don't belong there. . . . It's someone else's home." Scott looked to where he was going to be as he turned left into the parking lot.

"It's a nice place to visit, anyway." She shrugged and looked at the people walking on the paths that wound through greenery, which was probably mostly weeds in the desert offset by concrete. "What are we doing?"

"I think we need to walk a bit . . . stretch our legs." Scott swung into a space beneath a tree that was admirably struggling in the wind and heat.

She nodded her head and unplugged the player, replacing the cord with one that connected to earpieces. Scott stepped out onto the gravel parking lot and made sure that Lily scooted gently out of the pickup and had a good stance, before letting her go to shut the door and put the keys down into his pocket. He stood motionless for a moment, letting the morning sun feel its way over his exposed skin, reacquainting itself from his absence. A body pressed against his as he felt a dainty hand come to his face and slip something in his ear. The romantic, acoustic pop had returned. She slipped the player into the breast pocket of his button-up shirt, and then finally grasped his loose-hanging hand with hers. He looked at her and saw a look of determination on her face, trying to scan out the path she wanted to walk.

"Does it look like it'll work for our feet?" Scott tried to bring her focus back to where she stood.

"I don't know why the ground isn't paved with gold," she mused to him, gripping his arm as he led off.

"Our visit was kind of unexpected—"

"That's no excuse," she pointed out.

"And you would complain that there wasn't enough green if it was gold," Scott finished, as he felt her stifle a giggle.

"They should make it what I want," she declared.

"Before you know you want it."

"You get it; they should be more like you." Scott's face felt the sun in a different way as he smiled.

"I don't know that I should even be like me." He stepped to avoid a beetle that was crossing the sidewalk.

"I don't want you to be anybody else."

There it was. What she wanted and what she gave was support. The way she said "want" sounded like "need." Infatuation seems to grow out of a seed that you can't even see planted. One day a person just accidentally steps on the hard shell of minute life and unwittingly thrusts it into the soil. Nothing ever springs forth, that is, until like a beanstalk, it is an immovable part of the landscape.

"That's why I want to be what you want."

"You're so perfect."

"I want to see myself the way you see me." Scott broke them from the sidewalk onto the unkempt, dying grass.

"Think about how you see me." She waited a moment, then

hugged his arm. "That's kinda the way I see you." Scott crossed his arm to lay it flat on her back and hold her to him. She let go of him. He walked to the playground castle and sat on a platform an appropriate height for sitting. She moved around behind him and crouched with her hands on his shoulders. "What are you thinking about?"

"Things that make me hurt." A sweet voice that still encompassed hurt practiced falsetto in their ears. She wrapped her arms around his neck and set her head against his.

"Thank you for sharing your hurt with me. . . ." Lily thought for a moment. "A lot of people hurt because of people they love, but we . . . we share our hurt . . . and it makes me feel like I've found the part of me that makes things not hurt so bad. . . . I never want to hurt without you again. . . . You make even hurting nice. . . ."

Scott shuddered as the welled-up tears began to beat their way out of his tired eyes. His breathing ragged, she squeezed, and he felt her tears running into his hair. His eye felt immense pain from the exercise. Their bodies bucked against each other as they took desperate breaths in between sobs. Their eyes clenched because they could not let the person they loved and admired most see them break down. Their ears flooded with wonder at the thought of how someone could love one such as me; all the time so gone and meaningless until they found each other. Feelings change, don't they?

He was her plans, and she was his. Time wasted, but not youth. You the young in me, and I the smile you carry.

Thursday, The 13th
Late Afternoon

THE PICKUP SERVED SCOTT NICELY, THE ENGINE CATCHING IN the right places so that he could cruise at comfortable speeds without worrying about any cruise control function he typically avoided on vehicles. There was a country mile's worth of difference between the air conditioning he felt now and the mediocre one he had left behind. Most importantly, it was running and pulling him into the final American point of his journey. The city was heavy with cement and sweltered because of it, the roads open and ugly, and littered with automobiles of the spoiled and suspicious. No particular place in mind, Scott took turns on a whim and followed any kind of flow he felt.

Eventually, he caught sight of what he needed: a motel. The motel was not the first he had seen, nor even the first he considered, but as desperate as he was, this one more or less seemed to meet his standards. It looked cheap enough, though nothing was cheap anymore, and it looked decently clean—at least in a way that made him think that there would more than likely not be pest bites on his body when he woke up. He pulled into the lot, parking in a space off to the side of the office and out of sight from the main road. Making sure to lock the door, Scott made his way around to the front and entered through the standard commercial door on all older businesses. The vents screamed with the air conditioning, smelling faintly of cigarettes, while the desk clerk finished reading something on his boxy desktop monitor and looked up at the customer who had just entered. Scott pulled his lips into his mouth and bit down moderately and raised his eyebrows as his non-verbal greeting.

"Need a room, kid?" The old man rose from his swivel chair and leaned forward over the counter, sizing up the young man as if to pretend he wouldn't rent a room to Lucifer himself.

"Yeah, just for a night," Scott retorted, walking with measured steps to the counter where the old man slowly leaned away, sensing the uneasiness of his customer.

"Whole night?"

"Yes."

"How many?" The old man's question prompted an unthinking action of Scott looking around the room to see if he had accidentally brought someone else in with him.

"Just one," Scott answered, slightly confused, to the unimpressed old man.

"Look, kid, if I give you a room for one, I better not find any more than one in my room, got it?" The old man punctuated parts of his sentence with a boney finger tapping the countertop with force.

"I got it." Scott saw the seemingly no-nonsense approach of the man and decided to not take any offense, especially because it probably arose from experience.

"Good, because I don't feel like draggin' anybody out tonight."

"I hope you don't have to."

"Had to do it last night and the night before." The old man made it look like he was busy writing something and checking it against something else, but Scott doubted that it was anything more than an act so that he could keep talking.

"Oh, yeah?" Scott distractedly said, looking out the glass door to the cars flying by.

"First one was some fella that just wanted to shoot up and tried to cram six people inside after making out that he was the only one that needed the room." The old man continued to not shut up.

"How it goes, I guess." Scott was already tired of his voice and whining. Complaining was exhausting enough, but the worse kind was listening to it under the guise of the speaker grandstanding about their own abilities to overcome obstacles or acting in a way that tries to make them seem like the kind of person they wish to be perceived as.

"Other one was the typical fella and a whore—"

"Look, I just want a room for one for the night." Scott's patience had expired.

"Hold your horses, young fella." The old man grinned creepily.

"Sure." Scott looked around the room. The carpet looked like it had been cleaned but was still dirty. The fibers were flattened and filled with filth that could not be removed. He just wanted to get out of this room.

"In some kind of hurry?" The old clerk pried like Scott knew he would when he couldn't keep his own words to minimum.

"I'm exhausted and I want to sleep." Scott cocked his head. "I thought, maybe incorrectly, that a motel would be the place to fix that problem." The old man's face soured being confronted with a real no-nonsense approach that betrayed little extra information.

Scott paid the old man what the price on the sign hanging above the desk said and waited for the key. A displeased old man took the cash and picked a ring from the wall that held a key and a blue fob with the number nine printed in white. The clerk dropped it on the counter, and Scott, quite through with any facade, scooped it up and finished signing a fraudulent name on the ledger.

"Check-out is by 10 a.m." The voice was gruff, no longer being directly heard.

"Alright, thank you." Scott pushed through the glass door back into the heat of the day and wasted little time pulling the pickup around in front of his room. Scott hopped out and inserted the key into the door and stepped inside, flipping the light on. He took a deep breath. It would have to work, but he would need something first to set his mind at ease. Back outside with the door locked behind him, Scott pulled back into the road and retraced his steps until he came to the store he had seen on his original search.

Parking at the far end of the lot out of habit, Scott began his trek over the asphalt that felt like it was melting his boots. There were people exiting the store and getting into cars with foreign license plates eyeing him suspiciously like he was some kind of wild animal that was to be kept at a distance. Scott brushed off his dehumanization as he tried to step quickly to avoid the feeling of becoming sludge on the pavement. When he got near the sliding door entrance, he felt the rush of air from the store, and ignoring the possible formation of storm clouds at this intersection, he yanked a cart from the line and leaned against it, pushing forward into the grocer's arena.

The store was of a chain of a widespread nature because of the variety of products that seemed to have marginal differences in all aspects other than price. Atmospherically, the store was sterile and lacked any qualities that made a person linger longer than needed. The way the employees moved around instilled in Scott the sense that efficiency was top priority and that everything else would follow, or would become a nonissue with peak performance in their prioritized field. As their greatest nightmare, the young man who was just entering their store had no set list of items save for two.

Wandering, he passed the perishable fruits and vegetables, and made his way to the back of the store, perusing the cold items and pastries with no real intent to take any of them. With the aisles finally coming into view as he rounded the back of the store, he began to scrutinize the large signs which held the overview of the selection for that area. The first thing that caught his eye, as it always does for growing boys, was peanut butter. He procured the largest jar that was available and moved on. The next item, which, unlike the peanut butter, actually was on his list, was a jar of bay leaves that clunked into the basket next to the peanut butter. The next and final aisle he stopped at to complete his list and complement his food choice held crackers and another box of toothpicks to replenish his dwindling supply. His shopping rounded out, he located a line and stood in it, looking at all of the meaningless things scattered on shelves and wishing he had thought ahead enough to bring his music.

The person in front of him was a middle-aged, professionally-dressed woman who had an aura of tiredness similar to his own. She was either getting groceries after work for herself or for a family, either way not doing well to hide the stresses and tolls it took on her to be herself and an employee. With her arms cradled in front of her Scott could not see if she had a ring or not. The existence of that piece of jewelry being unknown, and with the trivial nature of the particular groceries on the belt, he could not really vouch for either possibility. No matter what, the situations were ultimately similar, and the only real difference was that if she did find a husband and have children, her stress would rise and her employer would see her as more of a burden: a vicious cycle of loneliness and neglect.

The young outlaw placed his four products on the belt and placed a divider to the rear of them for the man slightly older than himself who was behind him in line with products he was familiar with as a relationship-less male. The tired businesswoman kept her conversation and answers to idle questions short with the cashier, desperate to be out of the public eye. She paid and Scott approached the cashier when she had vacated the checkout lane.

She looked like someone he knew, or used to know, as was always the case from this point forward. She looked hard and uncaring in a way that was created to scare others before they could scare her. When she spoke, it wasn't soulless corporate-speak, even if it was small and idle. When she asked the standard questions, they seemed to wait in front of Scott and could be answered with a connecting gaze between the two people: communication without cumbersome words to be overheard by others and to be leeched away from their personal conversation. He tried not to stare, but he liked to be reminded. Even if she was not at all the person he made her out to be in his head, it was comforting to know that he knew someone once; to be able to describe somebody warranted a kind of intimacy that he had fashioned. Other people probably took it little into account how they were described or how they described people they knew, but it would always fascinate Scott. A fascination progressing into obsession. If he could not describe a person in a unique way, they were strangers to him, but the terrifying thought that haunted him was that if he heard a description of himself from a close friend, would he meet it with recognition?

Scott looked at the cashier girl and snapped out of his mind, her eyes showing fake confusion and real knowledge of his mind having wandered. She repeated the amount owed. Scott secured the money and counted out the bills to cover it. While he did this, he decided to stand out, a fool-hardy move considering his current status as "on the lam."

"If you had one wish, no tricks, what would it be?" Scott handed the money to a bewildered cashier who was not prepared for

114

anything other than small talk.

"I don't really know," she started, buying herself some time to think of what she truly wanted. "I guess I would wish for enough money that I wouldn't have to work anymore . . . or superpowers."

"Or superpowers," Scott repeated. "Why the money?"

"So I could do other stuff." She counted out the change. "And if I wanted to, I could get a job and quit anytime I got sick of it."

"Ah." Scott suspected that she could go into far greater detail, which would lead them down a road of talk that could last long into the early morning. "I would wish for a book with everything anyone has ever said about me." He took the change from her hand and his groceries and exited the building.

Rushing in a relaxed, inconspicuous way, he made his way back to the motel, pulling into the parking lot and cringing as he knew the nosy old man was certainly watching him get back from gallivanting. Scott took solace in not caring and the fact that there should be no doubt that he was reentering his room completely alone, so there would be no reason to disturb him. Propping the door open to the room, Scott transferred all of his things out of the pickup to deter any wandering eyes that might take an interest in what may be hidden and ripe for the taking in the small cab. The pickup was locked and secured with all the items transferred within the span of five or so minutes, and Scott closed the motel room door, locking it to its full potential. The curtains were pulled back with the blinds drawn, letting in just enough light for him to easily navigate the new place.

There was one thing he had to do before anything else, as he looked around satisfied with the items sitting on the table by the door. He reached into the plastic bag and grabbed the bay leaves, tearing away the seal and unscrewing the cap. He picked out a couple of the whole leaves, and holding them in his hand for a moment, he crushed them through the use of both. As he was about to sprinkle the bits near the door, it occurred to him that he wasn't very positive of where the trouble spots would be, so he ought to start around the bed where he would remain unconscious for a minimum of seven hours. The leaf remnants trickled to the ground where he dropped them, and he replenished his supply in his palm as they dwindled. Before getting too devoted to his task, he stopped himself and addressed his uncertainties, convincing himself that he had used plenty because he would more than likely be seeing the inside of worse places before his end.

No more work to be done, Scott undressed and rolled his clothes, shoving them into his duffel bag for future use and, hopefully, future washes. He entered the bathroom and tiptoed, slightly disgusted by the possibilities of the ghosts of things in the room. Standing in the tub, the shower was, thankfully, not so complicated that he struggled to figure out the proper use, so he found the temperature to be on the warm side of lukewarm and switched on the shower for it to stabilize before he stepped fully into the stream. His legs below the knee caught the water and seemed to find new life as the sweat was carried off and away down the drain. With the hint of steam starting to fill the air around his face, Scott stepped into the stream and used half of the provided products to clean himself as thoroughly as he possibly could without dipping himself into acid to be removed a clean skeleton, like a cartoon or an old horror film.

Scott shut the water off and toweled himself dry while still standing in the tub. After he had removed the layer of water from his body, he threw the towel over the curtain rod, pushed his hair out of his face, and stepped across the floor and onto the carpet. For some reason, the carpet felt cleaner than the linoleum in the bathroom, so he did not feel that standing on it was counter-productive to his shower. The sun was hanging low in the sky, as could be seen by the shade of hazy orange that illuminated the room through the blinds struggling to hold back the penetrative light of the evening. Dressed in a baggy shirt and a comfortable pair of shorts, Scott sat on the window side of the bed, leaning over the wall unit air conditioner. Fiddling with the dials and buttons, the unit turned on and began to blast the freezing cold air that he sought refuge in. He fetched the player and set the earpieces where they belonged and hit play on the one he wanted, sliding himself to lay in the middle of the bed with his feet off the edge and his head just below the pillows. The player lay silent next to him, but the cord carried the intermittent, melodic strum of the guitar as the orange light cascaded over his body, which still burned from the heat of the day and the subsequent shower.

After several days of being on the move, it felt heavenly to lie motionless in a bed with only about three quarters of his usual paranoia to nag him. His known vehicle had been traded in and the dash camera had been disposed of in a standing pond of water. While there were certainly a million mistakes and missteps to be counted, his body felt at ease. There was a tightness in his skin that had to mean that he had picked up a gradual sunburn on his trek across the state, but with the air screaming beside him and the coolness of the decorative side of a comforter against him, this moment in time would help. The ache of his muscles let him know that the pressure was alleviating, allowing things to let in the healing pain. With the dark blindness of closed eyes, old friends were allowed to be present and share the moment, to enhance the moment. With open eyes, he could know that he was all alone. What was new? Solace in solitary existence, maybe. Monks did it, he was sure, but he also did not know any monks, and while he would do a lot for what he believed in, self-immolation still seemed beyond his strength.

His hand wandered to the player. *Click.* The song began again. Just tell me what to do, but don't dare try to control me. It would be so much easier if she could just tell him that she never wanted or needed him. He would have never found himself in this mess, running and hated. The opposing mess would be dead and forgotten—choices that really made a young man feel confident in his decisions.

To be in the place where he fit was all he had wanted.

Sunday, The 16th
Evening

OUTSIDE THERE WAS A GRUMBLE OF THUNDER, PROMPTING SCOTT to open his eyes and see the barely visible ceiling of the temporary room that had looked down upon thousands of men and women and seen their stories. The dimness of the room resulted from the subdued grayness of the world outside, without aid from the artificial lights in the room. The depression beside him shifted, and her body moved so that she could conform to him and lay more fully against him. The rain came down hard against the roof of their room, pattering and forcing their heartbeats to stay steadily at a resting rate. The air inside had lost its crispness and had settled into the sweet smell of rain, which was seeping into the room and filling their lungs with the fresh feeling.

Analysis of the ceiling pattern proved to not be as attention-holding as he thought, and instead he cut his eyes to the side, only seeing a slight shape of her because of the limited ability of peripheral vision. She would occasionally twitch or move, but she did not make a sound. Without any snoring, he doubted she was asleep, but her breathing and the way she lay may have counteracted that. It was a shame that she was so silent, but any gentle noise of air being taken in or pressed out sufficed for the time being. Scott reached the arm not pinned by a young woman in love to the bedside table and picked the remote up, turning the television on.

The volume, already low, began to speak a distant Spanish to him while the light reporters read out the news to a man behind a camera. Pressing the channel button, he dwelled on different stations for short periods before moving on, curious to see if there were any that could actually communicate with him. He continued to flip through the channels but closed his eyes, letting his ears do the work and letting the rain-infused air settle on his numb eye. Finally, he caught a word he recognized: "Empire." Peeking his eye open, he saw the dated effects of an old documentary, revealing the topic of the rise and fall of Rome. Scott always found it perplexing that such a significant portion of human history could be boiled down to such an extent: never built in twenty-four hours, but easily explored in one. Despite this disconnect, Scott had a deep appreciation of things like this because all of this type of media chose different things to include. Different aspects became integral to the story of the greatest civilization to have existed depending on who created the documentation and when it was created.

One thing is constant across all instances, though: the men who led the civilization. Whether the documentarians condemn or critique, they cannot escape the power, charisma, and meaning behind the lives of these singular men. There may have been a ship that was Western Civilization, but there were memorable men who steered it to their own measures of what was needed. A man can only imagine what it meant and what it felt like to know that the world waited while he slept. And imagine Scott did, with daydreams and fantasies to be born and die in a time in which Roger certainly knew that the three of them belonged. Troy and

Roger had grasped the wheel if only for a moment and had been thrown overboard. Scott would not dare to put himself in the position of honor to have held it like they had, but he did not absolve himself of any action that occurred.

The air conditioner came on quietly, like an old man waking up at the break of dawn to go about work for himself, because there is no more work to be done for another, and to lie in bed while one's body still functioned was spiritual suicide. Scott thought about this as he lay in bed. The fulfillment of the circumstances became strained. Happiness lay next to and slightly on top of him, but the reality of his trend into complacency was becoming plain. It certainly seemed like a dishonor to his friends to live quietly with this wonderful woman. Even though they both would encourage it, the boat still remained on the course into guaranteed nothingness. Running, he had maintained the elation of action, but lying here with an unjust reward latching onto him like a medal he would never need to worry about misplacing, and listening to the stories of men who were long since decayed and returned to dust but continued to keep a gleam of admiration in the eyes of men who wished to be like them, he examined his place among the men great and unknown. Who was he? He could feel his spirit slipping. Everything he had done wrongly, everything he had not done, and everything that he had yet to do that hung suspended in the realm of "maybe" started to beat him down. Then, it occurred to him.

Every day seemed such a great unconquerable beast. One could ascend a mountain and, half dead, reach out for the hand of God from the peaks of the Earth, but the real battle was figuring out what to do afterward. Scott finally began to realize his madness. Waiting for moments would never push him forward. The chase of the moments and the subsequent capture was what he needed. There was no rest set aside for him. Each moment he rested, each moment he waited, was a moment he wasted. Yet with all that time gone and to never be recovered, he felt irreconcilably changed. In the mirror of his mind, a man he was barely able to understand, but always sure that he distrusted and despised watched him suspiciously; he was always wasting his time no matter who or what he was, never doing anything of note, and certainly not doing anything that would attach a good woman or wonderful friends to his existence. The outlier of his life turned and hoisted herself onto his chest as her glistening blue eyes fluttered awake, making sure the first sight they had would be of the man she could only love and admire. Her soft eyes discovered a sight that disturbed her innocent notions when she saw the horrors of life in his eye that was upon her.

"What's wrong?" Her eye widened and her brow furrowed.

"I don't know if . . . I can't really put it into words. . . ." Scott wanted to tell her everything he thought, but only half of the words he needed to say ever seemed to come to him, and never in a communicable order.

"What are you watching?" She tried to begin his venting or healing through an easier question.

"It's a documentary . . . on the Roman Empire." He glanced in the direction of the still presenting television.

"I'm not good at history, what happened during then?" She would not let his conversation die down. Scott blinked and felt thankfulness for her. Her admittance of ignorance and her subsequent question showed him interest and a willingness to learn the little bit he could teach. She did not pretend to know, like the vainly immature do, and she did not brush it off with admittance of lack of knowledge as if she was satisfied with that state.

"Quite a few things." Scott smirked and chuckled at his statement. "Roads were built that are still used today, lands were conquered and governed, people allied and betrayed, and eventually, it crumbled."

"Why did it end?" It only seemed natural to Scott that it would end, but stepping away from a historical perspective and putting oneself in the times of any civilization, why should things ever end? A day goes by and nothing major happens, he himself wastes his days, but he still exists. Entities, like the people that make them up, evidently can easily forget the mortality brought on by unforgiving time and change.

"I'm not a history expert . . . so answering that would just be my observations based on the little I know." Scott did not need to give her this caveat, but he felt obligated to simply out of hopes that she would grow and recognize the importance of limits as he had tried to show her.

"It's okay, you know more than me." She ran her hand over his upper arm.

"Just with Rome. . . ." Scott celebrated in being appreciated and encouraged, but outwardly he could only try to temper her view of him. "Overreaching. . . . It seems like . . . they made their home too big, and they couldn't keep track of it anymore . . . and smaller, more closely-knit groups could scatter them. . . . At least, that's just a guess."

"What do you mean 'they got too big'?" Lily posed the question at first in a way that seemed like it was born from low intelligence. Scott moved beyond that notion to see it for what it was: an inquiry directed at the manner of his meaning.

"I think they had too many different people pulled together." Scott tried to make things more clear. "It's like . . . did you ever play with the little blocks that connected to each other when you were a kid?"

"Not much, but I did when I had nothing else to play with" she said, trying to support his connecting explanation.

"Well, it's kind of like when you try to make a huge tower with all of the blocks at your disposal." Scott watched her captivated face. "But eventually it would start to get really unstable, because you were using different shaped blocks that didn't form an unbroken, simple shape. . . . Now that's part of it, but on the other hand, even with all matching blocks, you can spread them too thin for them to function like you need for the tower to stay together." She nodded her head slowly, wanting to say something. "What?"

"You look like you've been spread too thin," she whispered lovingly.

"I do it to myself." He cocked his head to fill in for an impossible shrug.

"I wish you wouldn't." She drew herself nearer, bringing her ear to where she could listen to his heartbeat.

"I wish I knew you when I was younger." Scott considered all the time that came before that was now wasted by her entrance to his life.

"You are young," she reminded him.

"I don't feel like it." He hated to be so negative.

"What does being young feel like?" She kept his mind working out loud for her to appreciate.

"It's . . . confusing . . . and hopeful. . . ." Scott chose the words he wanted carefully.

"Do you not feel like those things now?" Lily used her short nail to scratch at the intricately-woven, miniscule fibers of his shirt, creating a subtle, pleasing feel and sound to fill the pauses between their words.

"I still feel those things . . . but differently." It was always the same things, but different. "Mostly I feel . . . lost." He revised his planned statement before he finished, "And it hurts. . . ."

"I don't feel lost when I'm with you. . . ." she whispered, her insecurity telling her that it was her fault that he felt this way, that she was less than what she should be because she could not fix what should not be broken, nor remedy what should not be sick.

"I want you to be safe with me; I don't want you to worry about being lost, because I want to find the way for both of us." Scott reacted initially with pain at her assertion, assuming that it was to make him feel guilty, until he remembered who he was hearing it from, and seeing that the guilt was aimed inwards.

"I want to help you. . . ." Lily lifted herself over him, gazing down from her suspended view, her thin arms working hard to keep still, her baggy shirt creating a parachute between them.

"There hasn't been a moment that you haven't helped me since I met you." Scott lifted his hands to her waist and guided her down to the bed, shifting his own body to look down on her, his arms steadily planted in the bowing bed on either side of her head. "I feel lost in where I'm going, not who I'm going with." Her lips quivered as her eyes were flooded with the look of confusion of the insecure at immense kindness or love toward them. "You found me; now I want to find home for us." He leaned on one arm and touched her face with the opposing hand, replacing the hand to lower himself and plant a light kiss on her waiting lips.

Her hands wrapped themselves around his arms and buried her face into his left forearm, an action that was endearing to him, but about the purpose of which he was unsure. He did not know at this moment what she thought of him. Had she done this to hide her physical expression of love, or to show it? Had she come to the realization that she did not really know this man's life other than what he had told her or what she had seen? Was their short-lived world nothing more than that? The rain which, had quieted, began to again accelerate the rate at which it fell. Scott sat back on his legs and slipped down from the bed and leaned against the dresser that held the television, now at the point of Hadrian, seeking to hold onto the bursting seams of the empire that he inherited. Lily followed him, dragging the comforter behind her as she sat against the bed directly across from him, placing her legs over the top of his and bunching the blanket up behind her so she could sit comfortably, closer to Scott.

"Do you want to know something . . . ?" She whispered just over the low-speaking television, intermingling her voice with the pitter and patter of water from the sky.

"Yes." He lifted his head from its position lying back against the dresser to look at her, the insides of her eyebrows pulled upward in pure seriousness.

"I think you're my guardian angel," her voice returned, her eyes closed as she spoke in preparation to be derided.

"I . . . I'm not an angel." Scott tried to alter her view.

"You saved me." She opened her eyes, now ready to die on the hill she had chosen that represented the divine intervention of their meeting.

"I love you, Lily . . . but I just needed to get here without suspicion." Scott's words pained himself, yet Lily, initially recoiling at them, returned to her confident stance.

"I prayed for someone to save me that night." Lily was almost angry as she spoke. "And you did save me. You took me away from all of it and kept me safe."

"I don't know. . . ." Scott was uncomfortable as she seemed hostile at his revision of events. "I guess . . . maybe you're right. . . ."

"Why did you need to get here?" Lily looked fiercer than she ever had as long as he had known her.

He took a breath deep into his chest and held it for a moment before releasing it in an exasperation of having to finally speak his actions to another, to someone he loved; someone that he was terrified of losing. Lying was not an option. If she would hate him or love him, it would be through the truth. She would know the man that sat across from her, even if it burned everything they had built.

And so, he spoke of his actions. Some would label them sins, very few would label them heroic, and he would not label them anything other than things that he felt compelled to do through a combination of internal and external forces. He felt justified. He felt awful. He was not sorry. He only wanted to make things better. The countenance she wore had a million different emotions hidden behind her attempts to hold a serious, intent expression. He recognized disbelief and confusion and horror as he tried to tell her every single thing he could. What he feared most, her contempt, did not assault him. His heart still ached at his audacity to have existed outside of her. She had been right: things from before and after still mattered, and that moment on the beach was simply a memory now.

"I think . . . that's all." Scott tried to sit straight and look at her without wavering, resisting his ingrained habit of expressing shame after recounting events, and thankful that at least half of his face was still swollen shut. He kept quiet as she processed all that he said, giving her a moment to compile it all and respond. No less than two minutes of the television recounting the events leading to the fall and the rain becoming torrential had passed before she finally spoke.

"Would you do anything different?" Her voice was weak and cracking.

"Not a thing. I did it for reasons I still believe in." He paused and considered his next statement, trying to word it so that she knew it was genuine. "Anything I thought I'd change before now I don't want, because now I'm here with you." She could not look at him as she began to weep for reasons that were only known entirely to her. "Even if I no longer have you."

Lily clumsily got to her feet and tracked timidly deeper into the room, wiping her eyes consistently, expecting the tears to let up to

127

no avail. She stopped in front of the mirror and, through the dark, she looked at herself. Maybe she was reflecting on who this man was that had stolen her heart and given her his. Perhaps she reflected on the woman she was, criticizing herself for girlish visions of a knight riding into her world and blinding her with his heavenly light, glinting from his spotless armor. Or if nothing else, Scott prayed, she was considering what he said, and what had been said, and why they had ended up in this position. Turning, she entered the bathroom, shutting the door behind her. With light coming from beneath the door, Scott watched the manipulations as she stepped inside, the shower coming to life with a muffled spray.

Scott rose to his own feet and lumbered to his bag, pulling out the player and unwrapping the cord, placing the buds, once again, where they so often found themselves. The rustic roughness of Americana assaulted his ears and kept his mind alive as he fell back onto the bed. Honesty was such a wretched thing. There was nothing more honorable and universally loved and lauded. Sometimes it was easy but most of the time it was world-shakingly difficult. Scott always spearheaded things with the truth, but things never turned out as peachy as he was led to believe they would. People wanted to be lied to and that was something he was unable to do: just another disappointment to list in his docket of transgressions against his fellow man.

Poisoning the ground from which you hope to sow a lifetime and beyond of crops was not the way that had ever made any sense to him. If he took nothing else from insufferable French thinkers, he would certainly tend to his own garden. A lie may have kept her happy and sitting across from him the way he wanted her to stay, but he could not treat her the way the world had treated her. To him, she was more than what the world saw her as. She was herself, and nobody else seemed to appreciate that lately, at least not anyone that had the ability to reach out and hold her like she deserved. As she stood beneath the water, carrying the lumber of her thoughts down the river to the market of conclusion, Scott wanted to know what would happen. Like always, he could not know. Nothing was ever known. He had heard this song a thousand times before and he could recite the lyrics, but it sang something different to him each time. If he was lucky, the cascade of water, ripe with encroachment, would put out the fires of their world, would hold back the flames from the place their shared being reduced to the last gleaming ember.

He turned onto his side and looked at the gray sobriety of the world, plastering itself against the glass behind the blinds. How did he look in this light? He probably wore the doubt of the everlasting nature of her love for all to see. There could be no mistake made: if there had been a severing, it had been caused by his actions alone. As much as he wanted to put the decision on her strength of love, he had piled the straw on her back, despite knowing that she carried so much already. What he would not give to be able to see the future, to view his life in a way that would remove the tension of the stresses that plagued him. To him, not allowing things to hurt oneself was nothing more than indifference, and indifference would not infest his world, especially when there was someone to flood his world with love instead.

Eventually, the water shut off in the bathroom and Scott removed the lyrics from his ears in order to hear her shuffling around within the small room. Letting her dry in peace, he returned to the mud of melody. The artist proposed the possibilities hidden in the night, viewable only by the light of day, which remained far away as a person exists in the dark; reminding her of where she should be. Scott knew where she ought to be, but where would he go? She was out of his control, but his actions, from before and things to come, remained his. Where should anybody be? Obviously, the answer was home. After all that he had said to her, it became only too clear where home was.

The light from the threshold disappeared. Scott put the player on the nightstand and let his open ears be graced with her movement. The knob of the bathroom door turned with a small, slight noise and the door swung open without creaks. In the darkness, she moved in her heavy shirt, her hair in damp clumps against the colorless material. She approached the bed and stood at his feet for a few seconds. As if she could hide her movements, she crawled up onto the bed, straddling his body, leaning in to put her face inches from his.

"I'm yours." Her lips barely came into contact with his. Scott pulled her face against his.

"We're going home." They pressed their bodies into each other once again.

Tonight, they were where they wanted to be, and tomorrow they would be back where they needed to be.

HE WOULD NEED A SHOWER AFTER THIS. FINDING NEAT LITTLE treasures brought him joy, but the places where the treasures were stored were, in his mind, notoriously unclean. The word "thrift" itself carried a connotation of dirt and dust and the fragile shells of the empty carcasses of insects, even if the shop and items were relatively free of traces of their previous owners. Scott looked at all the items, some of them being obviously recognizable things, and others being absolutely alien cow tools to him. Evidently, they must have been dishware based on their surroundings. None of them warranted touching, just looks to take in the shape and color, and to inform speculations on the material before casting his eyes elsewhere to forget that they exist in any specified forms.

Looking over the shelves and racks of clothes, Scott caught sight of Roger looking at the section which contained knick-knacks, house decoration, and paintings. He was focused intently on a painting that Scott could not see except for the large, cracked corner of a frame that probably looked more expensive than it would be if people knew the materials that went into it. Troy was around somewhere that Scott could not spy from his current

131

position, but he had the suspicion that it was in a room sequestered off from the main floor so he could dig through the random junk that is tossed there because it does not necessarily fit anywhere else. Perhaps that's where all three of them belonged. Scott left the kitchen section and went to see what Roger was appraising, moving silently to his side, and taking in the sight. It looked to be a print of a famous painting of a park by a lake in the Victorian Period, the little dogs mid-run and the ornamented debutantes frozen in their delicately maintained version of beauty.

"Shopping for a new conversation piece?" Scott, now fully sidled up beside his friend posed this as a prodding joke, slightly accented by the necessity of his tongue to keep the toothpick in his mouth.

"Ah, not really." Roger turned his head to look at his friend, not realizing he had approached.

"Just admiring?" Scott pushed him to open his thoughts.

"I guess. I don't really like things that aren't original paintings." He shrugged, and jammed his hands into his pockets.

"That's a copy of an original painting." Scott smugly smirked, intentionally misunderstanding his friend.

"No, I mean that I like when people paint things, instead of just copy or make prints." Roger made clear his stance, knowing that he was being joked with, but giving his actual ideas anyway because he was not well-versed in banter.

"Why don't you like prints?" Scott scrutinized the image, picking out all of the small details, unimpressive and without exception on the smooth paper, but probably immaculate within brushstrokes.

"Because it's just done to sell things, I think." Roger was realizing that his views would not go unheard with Scott being in the mood that he was.

"Add them to the list then. But there's probably a lot of people that want those paintings to hang up in their homes."

"Those people should get real paintings. Unique ones instead of just posters of ones."

"What if they want those specific, famous paintings?" Scott was reveling in his success with his silent friend.

"They can go see them in museums." Roger was slightly frustrated, not with his friend, but with the individuals to which he referred. "Or buy big books with a lot of the paintings in them."

"I see." He looked around at the other art pieces on display.

"Why do you chew on toothpicks?" Roger's question put his friend on the spot, despite his meaning having no hostility behind it.

"I don't really know," Scott lied, having several ideas of reasons sitting at the forefront of his mind without thinking.

"I was just curious. Troy said it was because you were part beaver." Roger knew he was lying but did not feel betrayed. He was sure he had some of his own habits and thoughts that he would like to keep hidden as well.

"I like real paintings, too." Scott smirked and left him to peruse some more and walked to a shelf stuffed with heavy materials and dulled zippers.

Hesitancy stayed his hand from rummaging immediately because the piles of bags seemed to be stuffed so carelessly into the shelf, that to remove one would cause an avalanche of the rest. Scott scanned the ones he could see, trying to select the most likely candidate before trying to finagle it free to be inspected. There were many plastic backpacks for children depicting popular cartoon characters which had always seemed revolting to him. Playing on the immature delights and desires of children before they knew what was good, right, and necessary crossed his mind as particularly scummy and was thankful for his parents' general refusal of these inclinations when he was small. Any discontent he felt from not being purchased an item like that had faded away shortly after it occurred, as a whim did, allowing him to really develop a taste and eye for things that did not try to subjugate his personality through emotional toying. As he finally found a sturdy-looking duffel bag, removing it to give it a look over, he smirked at the thought of those that would accuse him of only holding the views that he did out of a lack of expression from oppression from guardians. But he knew himself quite well, and not through any television show, and that was worth it. The bag had a stain on one side, but other than that, it had no other issues, not even a faint smell of smoke. It was large, hefty, and perfect for his perceived uses.

Scott tucked the burlap container beneath his arm and wandered toward the mess of clothing hung on racks that was being browsed by a couple of elderly women. It baffled him to see these women here in what seemed to be the men's section. If they perused the button-up shirts or the children's section, he could reason that they were shopping for a grandchild or husband, but would they really be looking through t-shirts for either of those probable recipients? On the other hand, with the state of things being the way they were, they could be looking for grandchildren who were horribly obese and therefore could not fit in any clothes that one would find in the appropriate age section.

Seeing how thoroughly and violently they looked through the clothes caused him to turn away and try to ignore it. The action and effort they put into searching made him ache for a slower world, one where greed would ideally be less overall, or at least shameful enough to remain hidden. He did not want to dislike these absolute strangers, but it was difficult with how much of their personality he felt he could glean from simply keeping his distance and observing. There did not seem to be anything more to their movements, anything hidden behind their eyes; everything was just mechanical. Their own small little existence a blank space where they could build anything, but instead they chose a tiny corner and kept their stuff there, not concerned with the blank canvas all around them.

Making the world beautiful was hard, this is easily understood, but making oneself beautiful, on the inside and outside, is considerably easier. He wondered how beautiful the world would be because of him. He thought of all of the possible positive outcomes, but the negative possibilities were just as real, and pulled much harder than he could toward his fantasies. It was a frustrating time knowing that one was more than likely an example heralded as a reason to not be oneself. Learn questionable lessons from mistakes, never following an example. What a country.

Scott went away from the area and his thoughts to the rooms forming alcoves within the building, looking through the objects one never thinks about until it is seen. Boomerangs, crisscrossing shelves for wine, and porcelain mallards that seemed to actually be meant for a dinner table rather than floating on a lake to deceive all sat by one another as if that were naturally where they ought to be. The only objects which seemed to form any sort of community were the collections of books, primarily of the female fiction mongering sort to serve as a vehicle for one-minded women, and the ancient lines of VHS tapes that contained hours upon hours of films that had been forgotten in the collective sense. Scott scanned the tapes, some of the spines nearly impossible to read with the choice of font and being so worn, probably having been produced before he had been born. He picked one off the shelf and looked at the cover of a masked man wielding a knife red with blood and a half-naked woman trying to make an escape. Seemed good enough, so he continued to hold it and meandered to the shelves of books in front of Troy who was holding a large, flimsy one, the pages the off-white color that made one think of a modern classroom filled with the grating sound of workbooks too thick to properly write on.

"Is that Troy? With a book?" Scott approached him like a long-lost friend.

"Not just any book." Troy recognized the voice and continued to take in the larger titles of the spines. "One that requires a person to be able to read *and* think, so I'm afraid it's got at least two qualifiers that put it a bit out of your reach."

"I can sound things out," Scott suggested.

"I think I'd rather not hear you speak, so let's just say the 'sounding things out' option is a no-go," Troy said with a smirk, finally turning to his equally smirking friend.

"What is it?" He finally gave up the banter, recognizing the proper place to end the joke.

"Crossword puzzles."

"Crossword puzzles?"

"Yep."

"A book of crossword puzzles?"

"Mm-hmm."

"Used?"

"Only slightly." Troy grinned his stupid, pleased-with-himself grin.

"Only slightly." Scott shook his head, trying to hide his acceptance of the humor from his friend being intentionally foolish.

"Where's Rodge?" Troy looked to Scott.

"I left him over by the paintings." Scott pointed in the direction of the section.

"I'm about done. Get everything you need?" Troy watched Scott's face as he was now the one searching the books.

"I'm going to give these books the once-over and I'll be done."

136

"I'm going to go grab Rodge and get in line," Troy said, his bodyweight shifting as he subtly made the preparations to walk away from the spot he had been inhabiting.

"I'll meet you up there." Scott crouched down to see the literature on the lower shelves, taking in the comfort of books not of the romantic genre as Troy walked away.

Most of the titles were letter combinations he had not seen before with authors that may or may not have seemed familiar, save for a few. Of the few, his hand immediately floated to one and drew it out. It was a book that he would not consider old, but others, like the grandchildren of the two old ladies, would argue that it was ancient and probably archaic. Archaic, like he felt anytime he developed an idea or opinion about anything often a counter to what was the consensus. The book was flexible and had the natural aging that books can get, but there were not yet signs of cracking in the glue or pages split from the spine. He was not in the habit of rereading books, but perhaps this was the time that he ought to. This was a book that, from his memory, seemed to speak quite well to his current state of emotion and his appraisal of the circumstances in which he found himself. Maybe the last book he'd ever read. Scott stacked it on the tape and walked to the front of the store.

Troy and Roger were paying for whatever they had gotten as Scott approached the old man behind an open register. Neither said anything to each other and just nodded, fulfilling their roles as customer and employee. The old man moved at a speed that was appropriate for his age and strained to see the number on the screen in front of him when he had finished accounting for all the items. When he finished reading it out loud, Scott handed over the money that he had waiting in his hand for the man to finish. The young man placed his two loose items in the duffel bag and held it as the employee counted out the change and with a trembling hand, dropped it into a palm in much more working order than the deep creased lines of his own. Scott smiled and left the counter, walking outside where his friends were loitering by the door and watching for him to exit. With his arrival, they left as a group toward their vehicle.

"Let's go grab some lunch." Troy led the pack.

"I really need a shower," Scott broke in, feeling like he had gathered the dirt and grime from a million different people walking through a store of their stuff.

"Fine, princess, we'll drop you off. Right Rodge?" Troy turned as he walked and tapped Roger with the back of his hand.

"Actually—" Roger started, causing Troy to stop in his tracks.

"C'mon." Troy looked at him with disbelief until Roger started to smile and chuckle, revealing his misdirection. "You're real funny. I'm stuck with a princess and a comedian, no, a jester, yeah, because I'm a king." Troy beamed as the group surrounded the car.

"Yeah well, your liege, mind unlocking the door?" Scott yanked on the handle a couple of times, looking up at the sun, beginning to decide to swelter and cook the world below it as it rose higher.

"Exactly when a king means to arrive or whatever, squire." Troy was still pleased with himself at his allegory.

"That's wizards," Roger spoke, also starting to feel the heat and pulling lightly on the handle, "so hurry up."

"I will, just to get you two out of the sun, getting all hot under the collar and whatnot." Troy unlocked the doors and slid inside, starting the car and flipping the air conditioner as high as it would go.

The drive was short, the store being mostly a straight shot from one point to the other, and the topic of the conversation dwelled on what should be obtained for sustenance. While Troy controlled the conversation, Roger was the only one responding because he was going. Scott sat back and let them haggle, having no notion of a stake in the conversation beside what would be brought to him, and the mere fact that he was not accompanying them meant, in his head, that he had forfeited the right to ask for anything in particular. Troy, still weighing the options out loud, pulled to a gradual stop in front of the house. Scott stepped out into the street and went to the passenger's side window and waited for it to roll down far enough to hand off some cash to Roger who did not say anything but made a face that meant "see you later."

Up on the porch, Scott turned back to raise his hand to the car pulling away from the curb and accelerating down the street. Inside, he dropped his purchases, wallet, and keys onto the table in the main room, kicking his shoes into a corner where the young men typically left their footwear. He continued on to the bathroom where he turned the shower on and began to undress, stopping halfway and taking note of the silence and emptiness of the house. Taking advantage of his solitary surroundings, he exited the bathroom and went into the living room and dug through a cabinet which was seriously forgotten, holding remnants of times and technology long past. He pulled out a pair of speakers that would have plugged into a boxy computer that otherwise could not produce sound. Satisfied with the jack on the end of the cord, he retrieved his player and searched for the song he had had on his mind for several hours by this time, turning the volume all the way up and stepping into the shower.

The repeating strums by a learned hand could only barely be made out over the sound of the water pressured into thin streams hitting the porcelain of the tub. Human emotion through a New Jersey voice reverberated through the acoustics so characteristic of bathrooms. He would always remember and never forget. All of the filth washed away off his body as he felt his skin become slick with the clean-smelling water. Admittedly, the filth was almost nonexistent, just the hauntings of ghosts that leeched onto a person, touching the things that belonged somewhere until they did not. Scott washed himself with no real rush, slowing down as the lyrics replaced the old ghosts with ancient ones that filled his rooms of all of his life: ghosts of relationships that never panned out, of love that was meant to be but was turned against him through no fault of his own. Blaming himself served no purpose because to do it would just put him in the position of those he looked down upon: defeatists and self-denigrators. A sickness of the head. He ran his hands through his hair, pushing out the soap. This shower would not have the liberating effect that he had hoped it would.

Stepping out into the humid remnants of his action, Scott dried himself and let the song repeat, not letting the pain of thought subside. Whatever he would give to make things right would never be acceptable. Not enough pounds of flesh on his body to buy what had been lost to him and to his friends.

She would just stand mockingly in the outfit that had been bought and paid for already, and she screams how it, and he, isn't enough.

Monday, The 17th
After Midnight

THERE WAS NOT AN OFFICIAL MOMENT HE FELT HIMSELF WAKE, but there he was, awake and with awareness coming to him gradually. The room was silent save for the pitter-pattering of rain outside and above. The weight of a person was thrown partially over him. Her hand felt good draped over his body, each finger putting marginal pressure on his skin, but enough that he knew that it was there. She did not lose the magic one feels when touched and the position held. She did not need to shift constantly to remind him that she chose to touch him. It felt like she was satisfied to be there with him. To be on him.

Scott let his eyelids fall back down, shutting himself into darkness. The rain stimulated him. He wanted to listen to it, so his mind would not quiet, racing through nothing at all so that he could not fall back into slumber. He reopened his eyes that could now see clearly in the dark room. The slightest difference in his state of being must have disturbed Lily as she dragged her fingers closed and looked at him through tired eyes and with a yawn. Her eyes looked lost for a moment before the clouds in her mind parted and she remembered where she was. Who he was. Who they were.

She smiled at him. The rain slowed down.

"You're awake," she exclaimed in a happy whisper.

"I guess I am." His voice was low and quiet, trying to intermingle it with the muffled rain coming to an end.

"We both are."

"Why are you awake?" Scott placed his hand on the middle of her back.

"I don't know, I just woke up."

"Me too. . . . I'm sorry if I woke you up." He stroked her skin.

"Maybe we're supposed to be awake." She walked her fingers like the legs of a person over his torso.

"Why do you think that?" He watched her hand as he made his own still.

"Because everything feels still."

"It is . . . for us."

"Like it was when you told me about what you did."

"Lily. . . ." Scott started, but she continued.

"I want you to know about me. . . ." She sounded frightened.

"I want to know about you." He tried to soothe her worry with his solid statement.

The rain was gone. Its existence lingered in the air that seeped in from under the door and was attacked by the air conditioner in the wall. The only noise was now coming from the rush of air from the unit that sensed a warmer temperature than was desired. She rolled off of him to the distaste of Scott who felt unpleasantly alone without her feeling. Lying side by side and staring at the ceiling, Scott breathed silently, and Lily sighed and squirmed, finding the courage to speak.

"Now I see how hard it is to say something when you're afraid it might take something away from you."

"I love you, Lily."

She sniffled and lay still, wondering where to begin. Always so easy to know what you need to tell someone, but always so difficult to know where to start and how to say it.

"I never wanted it. . . ." She whispered to the dark, the depression in the bed beside her the only revelation of a presence to hear her. "I'm not a bad person. . . ."

Scott did not know what to say, nor when to say it. Was she saying that for him or for herself? He never once thought she was a bad person. He had thought often how he might be a bad person. Maybe as she stumbled her words out in that frightened tone, he began to understand her, to understand her in a way that she had already figured out for him.

"I know," he said, low and long for her to hear like the ghost of the voice of unconditional love speaking before cradling her from her worries of having sinned against what she knew, what she believed, and tiniest of all, herself.

"I knew a boy in my class," she began bravely, determined to get it all out. "Lots of people liked him. A lot of the girls liked him. . . . He was older than me. . . . It was an art class . . . something I liked and wanted to take and something he was just in because he needed something to fill his time. . . . We had to work on a project together, so he gave me his number so we could talk and figure stuff out with the project. . . . I—" she got choked up, unsure how to progress what she needed to say. "We talked . . . more than just for the project. . . . I thought I was lucky to have any of his attention. . . . He . . . he asked for a picture one night. . . ." She barely scratched out her words as she relived the regret and embarrassment of it all.

"Yes," Scott said, trying to sound sympathetic and give her something to support her fragile speech. Anything to confirm to her that he was still intently listening to everything she had the strength to give. Any wound she could reopen to clean away all that was rotting so that time may do its work.

"Not a good picture," she continued, "and I thought it meant he liked me . . . and I didn't want him to stop liking me. . . . I sent it for him. I *thought* it would just be seen by him."

He could hear the pain her face was surely showing.

"Lily. . . ." He didn't know what to say.

"He showed other people, and everyone found out. The school called home. My family found out. My grandpa found out. He cried and couldn't look at me. I hurt him so bad. I just couldn't stay there and hurt them . . . so I ran away." She was speaking through tears now. Scott intertwined his fingers with her and squeezed her hand. What was the use in telling her that they still loved her, that they did not want her to go away, that they never wanted to drive her away? It was impossible to convince a person that their existence was not an inconvenience to others.

"I'm with you," Scott whispered, squeezing her hand again.

"I went to the city. A man found me. . . . He put me up in this house with other girls. . . . He let us stay there and eat if we showed ourselves online. . . . The night you found me . . . that was my first night out. He had gotten angry with me and told me I was going to do things the old-fashioned way. I was so scared. . . ." Her body was heaving inconsistently with the ragged breaths of her sobbing.

Scott reached across his body and gently touched her arm. She threw herself over him and clung desperately, wiping her tears on his skin. She tried to speak, but she couldn't. He grabbed her and held her tight so she would stop trying to speak and just cry.

He couldn't remember the last time he had wanted to kill a person. He was angry so much of the time, and he had hurt people before, but the actual desire to end life felt fresh to him. Perhaps it's just the nature of the feeling. If anything would feel powerful and new every time it was felt, it would have to be bloodlust. His hands were far from clean. He had killed the Mexican a little over forty-eight hours before, but he did not hate the man. Maybe in a way there was a hatred for his actions and for his part in Scott's world, but the man himself was insignificant, just another event compared to the feeling that overtook him now. Whoever the boy was, whoever the man was, he saw them on the same level as himself, and he wanted to knock them down, to erase them for what they had done. A gift to man is the power to create and destroy: a power, not a game. These men, in the purest sense, played god. They lived in a surfeited world that gave them every opportunity to exploit and shrug off any person foolish enough to have faith misplaced in mankind, any person who, somewhere along the way, had forgotten their value inherent in being: the value that should cause growth to be even more, not to be bartered with.

"I want to kill them," Scott spoke in a pained growl, feeling her skin and bones and muscles and fat against him.

"No." She put her hand on his left pectoral. "I want to forget both of them. I don't want to see them ever again. If I could, I'd never think about them again."

"I love you, Lily."

She kissed his chest.

Her body had relaxed against him, her eyes still blinking away tears. Scott reached his arm to the nightstand and dragged the player onto the bed by the cords. He set one in his ear and the other in Lily's. He scrolled and located the song. Play.

An abusive acoustic guitar fought with the droning, traumatized voice remembering a singular time that crept up, when one can realize the worlds of others. A man is not a moon circulating me. He is something that will exist outside of me. The tree falls and I know it simply because it happens. My experience is not exclusive. The storyteller is merely a stop on the bizarre journey of another. Lily would not be a stop. Scott refused to be a stop. Their experiences would be intertwined like their fingers.

He closed his eyes and did not look at her. She closed her eyes and did not look at him. They could still see. They had to.

Monday, The 10th
Dawn

THE SUN WAS JUST PEEKING OVER THE HORIZON AND PEOPLE
were waking up to go to work. The car screeched to a halt in the
driveway, Scott pulling back as far as he could into the spot once
taken by the RV. As soon as the car was in park, he tore the key
from the ignition, his body from the car, and the player from the
seat next to him, slamming the door and running into the backyard
where he knew he would be able to find a covering. In the corner,
folded and disgusting from months upon months outside, sat a
large blue tarp, probably for a pool long gone, only the covering
outliving its components through usefulness. He stuck the player
in his pocket and grabbed the tarp haphazardly, ignoring the
probable creatures inhabiting the dank depths formed by the folds
holding onto old, stagnant water. Scott returned to the driveway
as out-of-breath as he had left it and thrust the tarp back to the
ground. Picking an edge, he yanked it away from the ground and
shook violently, trying to get it unfurled. Although not completely
open, the tarp was beginning to take shape, so Scott ran to the
other side of the car, pulling it roughly over the vehicle. He had to
obscure the world's view of it. Out of sight, out of mind, right?

The tarp covered most of the car, but Scott decided that the rear end, facing out toward the street, would be better to cover completely. He threw open the garage and fished out some bungee straps to counteract the wind of the Great Plains. He pulled the tarp taut and tight over the body of the automobile, strapping it to itself with the longer cords and to the undercarriage of the car with the shorter ones. If he was under any less pressure and stress than he was, he would almost feel satisfied with his work, but he did not feel that. He felt things indescribable and indecipherable at the moment. He lunged for the house with a long stride in case any of the neighbors were watching. His teeth were gritted harder than they had ever been before. It felt like they would shatter if he did not loosen up.

When he arrived at the door to the house, he fumbled with his keys, his body shaking and making the simple act of entrance into a chore that required all of his focus and a deep breath to calm himself. With the key inside, and turning the lock, Scott took a step forward, removing the key and closing the door behind him. He dropped to the ground, slamming his back against the door and forcing his hands into his hair. As much as he wanted to stop here and gather himself, he could not allow himself the chance. He unsteadily got to his feet and locked the door, undressing as he walked toward the bathroom, shivering as his mind tried to comprehend what he had been through. He ignored the silence of the bathroom as he stepped into the shower and turned the knobs on all the way and redirected the pressure to the head, letting the shock of the immediately freezing water cause him to jolt and pull away, but he jerked himself back and held himself, gasping beneath the water, his lungs struggling to work from the shock of the change in temperature. His mind wrought with horror and his eyes straining, he faced the wall and put his forehead against the cold tile, his hands bracing against the same wall. With a swift movement, his open hand formed a fist and slammed down against the wall. Scott swallowed. An exhale forced its way from his nostrils as the beginnings of tears.

He could not comprehend why, but his desire to put a hole through the wall never won out in his thought process. As badly as he wanted to do something, if he could not determine a net positive from the action, he would refrain. Destroying something for no better reason than to find a release for pent-up emotions would never be determined as something worthwhile. His hands lay flat against the tile wall as his breathing came under control and the water slowly warmed, soothing his body. His face stung, the water neither helping nor hurting the total dryness it felt. The hair of his arms felt wet and dirty now, so dusty that instead of washing it away, the water turned it into mud. Scott washed thoroughly, scrubbing every part of himself to remove the suffocating feeling that the skin gets when there is so much buildup of foreign materials on it. Eventually, the warm water and the active washing brought back the feeling of having pores unobstructed. He felt for any patch of body that had been missed, and having found none, he shut the water off and stepped wearily out of the tub, uncaring toward the puddle gathering on the floor beneath his body that now felt small and insignificant, like a lion drenched and shivering after a humiliating loss.

With the towel wrapped around him, Scott left the bathroom and walked into his bedroom, picking up the duffel bag he had recently purchased, and tossing it, open, on the bed, approached the dresser. He knelt down and pulled the bottom drawer free with the clothes inside all folded and prepped. He set the shelf on the bed beside the bag and began transferring the articles of clothing from the stationary container to the mobile one. The clothes fit well and left space for other odds and ends if needed, just as he had planned when filling the drawer previously. Previously when he

149

was bored and thought he should be prepared if he needed it, a thought without any real thought. His body was mostly dry, so he selected another pair of jeans and a shirt, pulling them on before putting on a pair of socks and his boots. Now he stood alone in all the world. Still a nobody, but someone that everyone had an opinion on. Mechanically, Scott left the room and went into the kitchen where he found his book, the bookmark waiting in the page where he had stopped. Beside it lay the book of crosswords, open and face down to hold the place. Scott stared at it for a moment, trying to reason if he was allowed to touch it, if it was disrespectful to touch it. He hooked his thumb under it and flipped it face-up and saw a half complete puzzle. What else had he expected? He suddenly felt stupid until his eyes caught one of the hints circled. A note, scrawled with effort to make sure it could be read by the eyes connected to the hand that wrote it, beside the hint read, "? Scott / Roger."

He hadn't known what he expected to find, but at least he found a voice. A decaying column of an ancient city as a reminder of a time long gone that would never ever return as long as the world existed, either his or in general. The numbness had already seemed to set in, the absolute disbelief that he stood where he did with things happening and having happened. He felt removed. He felt empty—the kind of empty that comes when one is abandoned by a person one counts on, not necessarily of their own accord, but it still feels like abandonment. With his book, player, and wallet from the pocket of his dirty jeans in hand, Scott returned to the bedroom and set the book on top of the clothes, as well as his wallet and player being set inside in similar positions, anticipating a long drive. He zipped up the bag and shouldered it, walking out of his room and into Roger's. There was so much he wanted to do, standing just inside the room, so much he wanted to say and feel. He wanted to give both of them a proper send-off. He wanted to honor their memories. He wanted to hurt more than he did, but he couldn't. They had given him so much and already lifted him, so that what he was left with was a hole that ached. He couldn't show all the emotions of loss because there were no emotions. They were gone; he understood that. He could not overflow with sadness because his sadness had been taken away with them.

Two worlds that had been bridged to his were now decimated. Nothing left of them except broken connections. Scott walked softly on the carpet to Roger's desk, littered with notes, books, and plans. He had to keep going. He opened the desk drawer and pulled out the revolver, sliding it into his waistband behind his back. Leaving behind his friend's former room, he closed the door, in his mind, preserving it. If he didn't think about them as gone, he could just convince himself that they were away, picking up dinner, and that they'd be back soon enough; however, he would not. These steps would be the last he would ever take in this house as far as he knew. This was a funeral procession for his life; the following days of his life would be spent cherishing every beam of it that shined through the darkness and avoiding the pallbearers.

Walking through the kitchen to leave all of that which he had known behind, he stopped in his tracks. Such a meaningless thing, yet he felt compelled. Old habits die hard for a lone survivor. Scott side-stepped to the counter and picked up the box of toothpicks. He shook it and only a few rolled around in the box, telling a grim tale of want. They would need to last, so he let them be and unzipped the bag, tossing it in with the rest of his meager belongings. Walking back out into the waking world, Scott locked the door and walked toward the older car they had left behind. He went around to the driver's side and unlocked the door, pulling it open. It felt unreal to be touching anything, standing outside with the sun now completely over the horizon and shining on him. The interior was not hot thanks to the time of day, but that played little part in consoling Scott. He sat in the driver's seat and tossed the bag into the passenger's and started the car. He didn't want to go. Not that he didn't want to leave, but he did not want to continue. He wanted to sink into the earth and be forgotten forever.

Scott closed his eyes and laid his forehead against the steering wheel. It was exhausting to have no motivation to move forward and leave things behind, to survive. His body could do what it needed to, but his soul was heavy. The emptiness was smothering it and preventing it from moving throughout his body. With no real change in mood, Scott let his body work without his defeatism controlling his physical abilities. He reached into the bag and removed the player, situating the headphones to whisper sweet or bitter anythings into his ear. The screen illuminated and he had no idea where to begin. The click noises happened slowly as he halfheartedly looked, landing on an artist he had neglected yet used to love. He opened their section and selected their first album. A song with a title that told him what he needed. The picking reverb of the guitar teased the listener. The artist knew that things did not feel right, felt empty. Scott shifted into gear and pulled away, thinking that he lost people he loved trying to make the world a place to love, too. He felt a little better.

Need any advice? We all feel alone.

Tuesday, The 18th
Morning

THE WIND WOULD OCCASIONALLY GUST HARD, HEADED SOUTH, and her hair would whip around, forcing her to close her eyes so she didn't get any inside. He would just hunker down closer to her to keep as much of the wind off her as possible, closing his own eyes to avoid her rouge hair as well. The parking lot of the roadside diner was mostly empty, being so early on a weekday, and Scott had just been thankful that they had been open from which to grab a nice, American breakfast. They both had had their fill and extra from the quiet people working inside. He surmised that they must have been the owning couple, probably working the entire restaurant themselves at slow hours like this one. Scott looked out over the rolling plains; a sight mostly unfamiliar to him. So much uninterrupted grass.

Another gust of wind howled into them, Lily bracing closer into his denim jacket until the wind had ceased its attempt to pick her up and carry her away. He felt real. Not necessarily free or without concern, but a sort of legitimacy that made things seem a lot closer. The world wasn't closed in on him, but it felt smaller, like the world was no larger than what he could see. Turning his head, he looked at Lily. Of all that existed, they did, and they were significant. Their actions and words and thoughts meant something. They were not washed away in a Malthusian nightmare. The scene was a freshly-painted landscape, and they were part of it. They did not need to be the focal point, but eventually one's eyes would wander to them and appreciate them like the infinite grass or a lone tree.

"My face feels dry," Lily said to his abdomen.

"It might be getting wind-burnt. Do you want to go inside somewhere? We can go ahead on our way." Scott talked to the top of her head and tried to push off the front of the pickup to guide her to the cab.

"Not until you're ready." She stayed against the pickup, her body extending as he leaned away from the position she was determined to stay in.

"I'm ready if you are." He wanted her to be comfortable.

"I'm not; I want to keep looking," she spoke again into his jacket, obviously having none of his self-sacrifice.

"Then I'll keep looking, too." He was head over heels for her at this stage of knowing her: a woman who refused to put herself first and would go out of her way to make sure that she wasn't sneakily being maneuvered to the front of anyone. Scott loved the thought of her actions, even if they were less thoughts and more ingrained personality. She was good despite all that had ever happened to her.

"What's the world like?" She asked like she did not know. Perhaps after meeting him, she didn't.

"I don't know. . . . I can't be sure the right way to answer that, that is to say what you're asking, and even if I did know, I don't know if I could answer." He gave her a non-answer without thinking, and after reviewing his own words and feeling her breath into him, he began again. "The world is everything. . . . It's the moments when we have to do things we don't want to do, to the moments when you have to cry over the people that aren't in the world anymore, to the moments when you're sitting on a beach with the person you love but you're both too afraid to admit it." She squeezed his arm. "To the moment when you feel like everything you knew about a person is shattered. . . ." He trailed off, thinking about the last moment.

"Yeah?" Lily looked at him and his eyes locked with hers, her hair blowing in strands in the same general direction across her face and her eyes radiant blue, like the sliver of untouched sky between the clouds that were the gallant chariots, the signature of the Western vistas.

"To the moments when you're lost and just trying to find a place in the world so you can feel like you've felt what the world was like." Scott could not escape the beauty no matter where he looked.

"Thank you for talking." She looked out into the distance where the buffalo used to roam in a different world.

"I know you listen. . . . I just need to remember that before I don't answer," Scott admitted, thinking of the times he did not speak to Roger or Troy.

"I do more than listen." The way she could say things that knocked his intellectual legs out from under him would never cease to amaze him.

"Do you think of me differently since I told you?" Scott hadn't yet asked about what she had thought about when she had gotten up and walked away in a moment that seemed like a million years ago.

"I didn't know what to think at the time," she began, her voice unsettlingly steady. "I felt like you lied to me at first, but the more I thought about it, I knew you didn't do that . . . and I couldn't believe you did it, but I also thought about it and it makes sense. . . ."

"It makes sense?" Scott needed to know which thoughts she was having or what words he said made sense.

"It made sense that you would do it, especially after all you told me." She craned her head back and closed her eyes. "I even think all of it makes sense."

"Do you really believe that?" His eyes were focused on her perfect face.

"I'll believe anything you tell me." She smiled and opened her eyes, her eyes already his direction.

"I wouldn't lie to you." Scott wore the pain of sincerity in the dark areas underneath his eyes.

"I know." She turned to him and leaned in, planting a kiss on his chin.

Somewhere out beyond his sight were all the answers he had ever thought he wanted or needed; at least, he used to think that. It seemed like the more he learned, the more he realized that the answers were not running from him, but they were hiding. Plotting out the journey ahead, he couldn't waste his time chasing or searching; he had to make things the way they should've already been. Sometimes a man has to do it alone; most of the time a man has to do it alone, but he was thankful that he had a piece of himself with him to help and follow. He took Lily and led her into the cab on the passenger's side, as usual, her using his trek around the front of the pickup to scoot into the middle of the bench seat to wait for him. Scott opened the door and took a last, still look at a sight that was not the same as yesterday and would not be the same tomorrow. Change may be inevitable, but a man has the strength and will to resist it. Death was also inevitable, and men continued to live. He would leave the quick and easy path to the inevitable for the weakened rats living in the utopia. He still loved her and would fight for her, but Lily was here and now, and that woman had done more for him than *she* ever had.

Inside the pickup, with the doors closed tightly, the wind would jostle the vehicle and would scream against the windows. It unnerved the two slightly, but then Scott, for no reason he could know, laughed. The wind rocked the truck, and he laughed. She looked bewildered, then she began to laugh too. It just came naturally. Neither Scott nor Lily had a clue for what purpose they were laughing, and that just made them laugh more. Lily picked up the player as Scott started the pickup. While she was trying to look between her convulsions, Scott gently took the player from her and scrolled to look for a song that he hadn't been able to listen to since he was a kid: one of the most popular musicians of all time and a dearly loved song, a song about the love that gave him hope as a little boy, but it began to serve as a kick in the teeth as he grew. Now he felt good, and he wanted to hear it with her. The western instrumentals and the pure voice took them both back.

He took her hand, they took their thoughts on love and how it goes, and they headed for a home they never knew.

Monday, The 10th
Early Morning

THE DARKNESS WAS STILL, AND SCOTT STRUGGLED TO STAY awake, focusing on the music playing loud enough that he could live the songs but low enough that Roger beside him could nap if he needed, which he did. There wasn't much farther to go to their destination, he guessed, looking at the time. About twenty minutes more and he should be pulling into the city. He looked in the rearview mirror and saw the RV following a few hundred feet back with Troy at the wheel. Scott made sure to keep him in sight just in case either of them came upon any problems. The highway was empty except for their two-car convoy and the occasional eighteen-wheeler headed the opposite direction. Scott felt the toothpick in his mouth and knew he was nervous because he needed another. He removed the wooden spear from his mouth and was about to drop it in the cup holder when he had an idea that made him grin.

He glanced over at the sleeping lump that was Roger and saw the breast pocket of the plaid shirt he wore over his t-shirt. With the mischievous crinkle around his eyes, he shot his eyes between the road and his friend as he slipped the used pick into the pocket.

He blew air out of his nose in a muffled laugh and replaced the place in his mouth with the last toothpick on his person. Scott yawned and turned the volume knob for the music upward in two increments, hoping that it would grant respite from his tiredness and not wake up Roger.

The speakers fluctuated wildly between folk ballads of personal experience to fantasy synth to harsh, pleading rock. Scott easily adapted with each change, feeling all of them on a level that he really shouldn't have. Each note a little man standing out on the surface of his own world, a king of nothing and everything. He had probably already thought that. The problem with thinking so much is having the same thoughts over and over again with little variations or a different perspective. Each thing may be significant to him, but it's just a broken record to everyone else who did not have some sort of degenerative memory as a consequence of staying too long in one's own head. Not to mention the self-criticism that beat every new idea mercilessly. Being awake at such a forsaken hour granted such clarity that would make it a much-loved time if not for the simultaneous hallucinations. Everything was too quiet in hibernation. There were so many dreams traversing through the dead air that one can't help but get mixed up. One could laugh or be overtaken by sadness, depending on which wandering dream one runs into.

Maybe it was a change in chord or a bump in the road, but Roger fluidly stretched into an awake position, loosening up his joints and looking out into impenetrable night. Scott saw the return to consciousness from his friend, but kept his eyes forward on the droning highway, not saying anything that would slow his grasp of remembrance of his situation. Roger looked back at the headlights following and then to the dense brush rushing by on his side of the vehicle. In the distance, a glow of an urban center polluted the sky with its beacon of what passes for civilization.

Roger sat back in his seat, moving like a person now fully awake and present to keep Scott company for the last leg.

"Good morning," Scott yawned.

"Not too far now, is it?" Roger could certainly see the glow.

"Probably only ten or fifteen more minutes." Scott shifted in his seat to help his body maintain its alertness.

"Thanks for driving." Roger rubbed his eyes.

"Don't mention it." Scott lowered the music the same two notches, preparing for further conversation.

"How are you feeling?" Roger asked, the question either being a normal continuation of the talk or a bona fide check-in of his mind and heart. Scott, seeing the short few minutes before crossing into the outskirts of the city fast approaching, chose the latter possibility.

"Nervous again." Scott kept his response close to his chest.

"I think we all are," Roger spoke, and Scott could not tell what his tone meant; it betrayed nothing to the listener.

"How are you?" Scott glanced to his passenger, looking exhausted and stressed through the window and hoping for an answer besides an obvious one.

"I was alone a long time before you guys came along." Roger was watching the blurry mess of mesquites and caught tumbleweeds on the side of the road out of his window. "What I mean is that I don't suppose it was a long time, but I was really alone, and I was scared." Scott remained silent, staring at the yellow line lit by his lights. "We all found our way to where we were, and what we thought, and I suppose that made us feel even more isolated." Every brief pause was filled by the honeyed sounds of another's misery, artistically showcased through the speakers. "After my parents died, I kept the . . ." Roger trailed off in a way that had been predominantly reserved for Scott's mannerisms.

"What did you keep?" Scott was monotone, unsure how to

161

react.

"I kept," Roger began loudly, and after a sigh, softly, "the family gun." He stopped only time enough that he realized he did not want to expect a response yet. "In my desk. And occasionally I would pull it out and let it sit there, I don't know, maybe expecting it to talk to me."

"And it didn't." Scott bridged the implications.

"No, it didn't. Apparently, I'm not crazy," Roger chuckled as he thought about it, finding humor in his actions in some of his darkest times.

"I don't have a gun story . . . but I've got another story . . . and I'm sure if you asked Troy, you'd see his face drain . . . because I bet he's got his own, too." Talking about things like this scared Scott. It gave him an unabashed feeling of self-recognized weakness that stung him as he said it to a friend that had opened up about the same thing and who he did not see as weak.

"We're doing this so there aren't so many stories like ours, then." One could hear the resolution returning to his tone.

"After we do this, people are going to think that inanimate objects talk to us." Scott did not know why he only had jokes come to mind when he certainly didn't need to be joking.

Roger looked at Scott and smirked, appreciating the black humor that diffused the tension. If Scott felt confident in his people-reading abilities, he might guess that his lack of emotion helped Roger's confession. A lack of reaction meant there was no reason to go on any tangent of justification or absolution, just to speak and listen and to say things as they are without care for their content so far as one could respond. But that again was Scott's own fantasy of being better than he probably was. Roger looked around the car at nothing in particular and rearranged his sitting position to sit straighter like Scott had previously done. While doing this, he tugged on his plaid overshirt by accident, pulling it tight against his chest. His face immediately grew confused. He held himself up and kept the shirt pulled, moving it scientifically to see what was off about it. Certain of where the issue was coming from, he sat back in his seat and began patting around on the left side of his button-up for the strange object, eventually reaching his pocket. Seeing how the shape fit within the stitching of the cloth holder, he stuck two fingers in the pocket and searched for whatever it might be. Feeling it with his fingers, he began to understand what it was. His head whipped toward Scott and his eyes narrowed.

"That's gross." Roger smirked and shook his head with his eyes set on the side-profile of his friend.

"Careful, there's a mirror on that side of the car, some pretty frightening sights there if you happen to look in it at the right angle," Scott said, pretending to be ignorant of what Roger was referring to. Roger blinked slowly and pursed his lips.

"I thought I was supposed to be the comedian and you were the princess." Roger sat back, leaving the toothpick in his pocket.

"That would make Troy right, and then Troy would be a king, and is Troy a king?" Scott posed to his friend now considering the implications.

"I guess if the kingdom is filled with a bunch of donkeys that more often than not lead with their back end, then yes," Roger asserted.

"You got me. With us in his court, he's certainly on that track." The city lights had not only approached, but the brush had cleared away and the sprinkling of urban sprawl was beginning to rear its hideous and "dynamic" head.

Putting hats on and pulling them low over their faces, Scott pulled the car into a gas station to top off the tank. Scott got out and waited for the pump to be ready while Roger walked into the store to pay. As the pump became ready and Scott pulled the nozzle free, Troy pulled the RV into the lot behind him and hopped out, walking up to his gas-pumping friend and stretching out his limbs.

"You should probably put a hat on, just to make it harder to identify you," Scott pointed out from behind his toothpick.

"I'm not worried; the cameras never show much of anything, besides two more reasons." Troy was evidently focusing on his confidence rather than letting his nerves get to him. "We'll be scarce after this, and I look pretty generic."

"You have it all figured out, don't you?" Scott looked at Troy and then over to the store where Roger was exiting and coming toward them.

"I have about as much figured out as you do, and that's why we're here." Troy got Scott's attention back on him as he was met with subtle nods of agreement. Roger stopped on the other side of the vehicle and peered across the top at them.

"Where's your hat, Troy?" Roger chided him.

"It's a whole thing. Messes up his hair; don't get him started." Scott answered for him as Troy's mouth hung open in a smile ready to go through it again.

"Well, I guess we can decide now if anyone wants to turn ba—" Roger did not finish his question as he was harshly cut off.

"No," Scott said without thinking, not allowing himself or his friends to be held back by self-doubt after they had all already meditated deeply on the matter.

"No from me, too." Troy spoke much slower, looking thoughtfully between the two men he was intrinsically bound to.

"Then we're all ready." Roger was unsure of what to say after the shock of being cut off by Scott.

"I wouldn't go that far." Troy lightened the mood only to bring it back into seriousness, "but we all know we have to do this."

"Let's go." Roger was now the pulling force. "The more we wait the harder it will be to get done."

The gas pump clicked off as the funds provided ran out, and the young men piled back into the vehicles, this time Roger with Troy in the RV and Scott alone, following them. They drove away from the oppressive night to the artificial daytime of a nighttime city, deeper through the streets until they neared the urban center with its empty office buildings and sleeping government buildings. Scott kept a block and a half between him and his friends until he saw them pull closely to the curb in front of the building they had been heading toward. He parked the car at the end of the block one block away from where they had stopped, shutting the engine off and putting on the parking brake. He exited the vehicle and stuck his hands deep in the pockets of his denim jacket and walked along the sidewalk toward the RV. The streetlights hummed in the quietness of the world, his boots making distinct noises as they struck the sidewalk. On his final approach, he slowed down and looked around, gazing up at the building to his right. There were seals plastered on the door and a being who was a criminal and a degenerate as far as Scott was concerned encased in bronze: a dead-eyed, mouth-agape, apt mascot for the monument to the decadent disgust toward the past.

The building rose six stories into the sky and housed agencies that created their own problems to fix. They were groups and coalitions that created the new face of a coin each time it was flipped, nothing more than weapons of a select few, who could hardly be considered elite, to strike at anyone that decided to not be steamrolled. They actively spat on any man who dared to be a man, and despised anyone who dared to remain what God had made him. Scott felt his anger tingling through his body. He turned away and entered the RV through the door on the side. Both Roger and Troy, busy at the rear of the cabin area, turned to look from their kneeling positions at the person who had just entered. Troy continued to look at Scott while Roger had turned back to continue working. The setup laid out before him was completely foreign to Scott. He had contributed in countless other ways, but Roger working diligently and Troy still looking at Scott were the two concerned with the actual engineering of the plan.

The empty office buildings set Scott at ease, but the building next to where they sat surely would contain material that could only help those who deserve contempt. They were certainly counting on the spectacle to play in their favor: defacement of the hideousness that plagued their lives and the lives of others. Scott finally made eye contact with Troy.

"What?" Scott could not pose the question any way that would not sound harsh and pointed.

"What are we doing?" Troy pleaded with Scott.

"You know what we're doing." Roger finished doing what he needed to for the moment and looked up at Troy, who jerked his head to look at him.

"We're doing something to show the people trying to kill us that we're not dead yet." Scott leaned against the cabinet forming part of the kitchen area, chewing his toothpick slowly and carefully, the power of his anger resonating in his jaw.

"Not dead yet," Troy repeated, Scott walking toward his friend exhibiting real fear.

"For our fathers." Roger turned back to his work. "And for their children and the men that come later. For all the names we know and all the ones that won't ever be named." Troy looked at the tool in his hand like it did not belong there. Like none of them belonged there.

"People are going to hate us more than they already do." Troy set the tool down and put his face in his hands. He felt his friend walk away from him, so he looked up to see Roger looking toward the front, following his friend's gaze to his other friend. Scott threw the door he had come through open and pointed outside with his friends looking up again, waiting for his words.

"When a man like me a decade from now asks how it got so bad, why nobody did anything—" he turned his head to look at the ugly statue. "My conscious is clear. We did something." His body was unmoving, but each limb felt something different than the one it was connected to.

"You two are the best people I've ever known." Troy was crying.

"The world we know can hate us, but we have the world that always was and, more importantly, each other." Scott shut the door and sat on the ground, tired. After a short period of reflection, Roger broke in.

"It's all touching, but this is almost done, and when this is done, we need to be gone." His face was red and worried, and his entire body was drenched with sweat.

"Alright, I'll go keep the car warm." Scott rose to his feet and kept an eye on his friends, noticing that both were drenched in sweat, hunched over the device. He could not see Troy's face from the angle, but he saw his head turn to look at Roger who had a grave expression.

"Hey man, I really meant it, best guy I've known," Troy said, still facing away.

"Yeah, you've always had a soft spot for your clowns and princesses," Scott shot at him, avoiding another tender moment.

"Yeah, yeah, just do me a favor and jog because we are about done and I don't want to hang around. Don't let the door hit ya on the way out," Roger stuttered out with a smile that seemed odd.

Scott cocked his head and furrowed his brow in confusion at the different way of communication that Roger was attempting, but he decided to not distract them any longer and exited the RV. He did not know if Roger had been serious about the jogging, so he jogged anyway toward the car, traveling on the asphalt of the street directly behind the RV toward the front end of the car. The air was not clean; the air of the day was still rife with fumes. Approaching the car now only a few yards away, Scott slowed his speed to a near stop, turning with his last bit of momentum to see where his friends were.

The shockwave shattered every window in the vicinity and tossed Scott onto the roof of the car, bouncing off onto the trunk and then sliding off the trunk limply with a thud onto the glass-speckled ground. Scott raised himself up onto his elbows and stared ahead at the curb. He instinctively laid his hand down before withdrawing it immediately, having felt the glass littered all over the ground. Like a drunkard, he rose, carefully touching the car, and trying to avoid lodging any glass into his skin. He stumbled backward away from the vehicle, almost falling but managing to save himself. He touched his ears and didn't feel anything wet, holding his hands out in front of him to make sure. There was a distinct lack of blood. A miracle. He looked up at the crater and raging fireball that used to be his friends. He took two running steps toward the lifeless entanglement of metal and the shining tar of the street before coming to a halt.

They weren't there. They were gone. It was just him and his world again. It had been done. He wasn't dead. He wasn't dead yet. He backed away hesitantly before turning and rushing to the windowless vehicle. He yanked the door open and used his denim-clad forearm to sweep the glass off the seat into the floorboard. Hopping in, he started the car with a prayer. It came alive. Another miracle. Two tragedies for two miracles, he supposed. Anything more would just be gracious mercy. As he cut the wheel away from the curb and pulled the car in a sharp U-turn, he noticed that he had neglected to stop the player. A panicked guitar began before giving way to an arena-filling beat. The voice returned: reminiscent of youth, from before the bad times. Scott pressed the gas pedal deeper and deeper, trying to touch the road. The wind whipped though his hair and carried the dirt from a dry land into his face. His world was under threat and he, without allies. Desperate. He just wanted something he knew was possible. Why had people let it get this bad? Why did he have to do something? Just another love song for something or someone from a world isolated.

He never had it, and he could never get it back. He just wanted it back.

9 781956 887648